The Happy Few

RACHEL-ÉLISE CAIRNCROSS

ISBN: 979-8-8650-7699-5

DEDICATION

For my wonderful family with all my love.
And for everyone who helped bring this story into being—thank you.

CONTENTS

"Whether it be that the multitude, feeling the pangs of poverty, sympathises with the daring and ingenious depredators who take away the rich man's superfluity, or whether it be the interest that mankind in general feel for the records of perilous adventure, it is certain that the populace of all countries look with admiration upon great and successful thieves."

- Charles Mackay, *Mémoires of Extraordinary Popular Delusions and the madness of crowds.*

PROLOGUE

In a chest in my room is an old letter. Faded yellow pages covered with browning ink are stacked one on top of the other and tied tightly with a red ribbon. The pages were written long ago, but the ribbon is mine, added to the stack in a fit of sentiment. I've always been prone to sentiment, though I fight it when I can. My Grandfather once told me that it is my most endearing quality—make of that what you will.

The first time I saw this manuscript, I barely dared to breathe on it, never mind wrap a ribbon around it. Over time, my caution wore away, as the pages became more familiar to me, and their words settled into my heart like the memory of an old friend. I can envision the scenes that play out in this letter as clearly as if I had witnessed the events with my own eyes. It takes no effort of imagination to summon up the image of a woman sprawled upon cobblestones—her desperate shout drowned out by the roar of flames consuming a house behind her. There are nights when my dreams are filled with the pounding of hooves, the crack of a pistol, and dark phantoms falling to the ground. Five faces are enshrined in my heart. Although I have never seen them myself, their features are as clear and familiar to me as those of my own family. I feel that their lives have unfolded and faded away before my eyes in beautiful, terrible glory.

I have loved this letter my whole life but treated it with as much careless familiarity as one would any beloved book. The culmination of this familiarity came one evening as I sat in my favourite armchair, swaddled in a blanket, tissues in one hand, manuscript in the other. Unwilling to drag my eyes from the words even for a moment and risk pulling myself from the familiar world my mind had strayed into, I reached for a mug with one hand and succeeded in spilling its warm contents all over my lap.

The damage to the pages was minimal—a pronounced wrinkle in one corner of the stack is the only remaining testament to my foolishness, but it was enough to push me firmly back into the realm of caution. I treat that stack of pages more like a relic than a book nowadays. It resides in a chest in my bedroom and rarely sees the light.

The author of these pages has always been an object of curiosity (and I will admit, romantic sentimentality) to me. As a child, I imagined her sitting at a desk very similar to mine, writing on pages illuminated by the early morning sun. A long letter such as this would require hours of daylight, or so I assumed. I occasionally imagined that the author preferred candlelight. Words are so often secret things passed from heart to page, so perhaps the darkness, broken only by a small, flickering light, would have helped the memories to flow more easily. Now, I prefer to picture the author basking in the afternoon sunlight. The morning would have been dedicated to contemplating the task ahead, and then the writer, fortified by a light lunch and kept company by a china teacup, would be ready. Her pale hand would have hovered above the page, a beautiful blue stone clasped in silver adorning one finger. Now, she takes a breath, gathers her thoughts, and begins.

CHAPTER ONE

Dear Mr Simmons,

When we last met, I mentioned that I was interested in relaying to you an account of the life of a well-loved friend. It is a story of some interest to many, though that interest is now fading. I hope your company may find it enlightening and, hopefully, publishable. This tale has always been very close to my heart, and I understand that you have invested a substantial amount of time in researching portions of it. I do not doubt that you have heard many versions of this same story, but I ask that you do not immediately dismiss this one. What sets my version of this tale apart from others of its kind is that it is true. I endeavour to disclose to you, in every aspect, as accurately as possible, this account of Frayne's life.

I must admit, I don't quite know where to begin Frayne's story. It is a common rags-to-riches tale, but with all the pain that reality can bring to bear. Frayne's mother (if I can even use that word to describe Trudy) was an unfortunate woman who spent her life in a constant state of displeasure. Since she was never happy, then why, I am sure she asked herself, should anyone else be happy?

Trudy was short, round, and red-faced. Her apron was permanently stained, and the cap upon her head was incapable of containing her strands of greasy hair which, though limp, seemed to have a mind of their own. Once, Trudy could have been beautiful. Her hair was dark and if washed, might have held a hint of a curl. Her eyes may have been a striking blue beneath the blood spots, and her mouth full were it not forever compressed in anger. Perhaps this is all romantic imagining. No one who knew her could have ever seen these hints of beauty in her, no one perhaps but her son.

Trudy made her living selling fish. Each day she would lay out her wares with a grim determination, then shout at passers-by until her fish had sold, at which point she would return home. Coarse and loud, one would expect that business would be hard for Trudy to come by, but the opposite was true. Trudy was dependable. She had been selling fish for as long as most people could remember, and many believed that she would keep on selling fish until she was dead and in the grave. People like what they know, and in that town, everyone knew Trudy.

With a reliable source of income, Trudy might have done quite well for herself, but her ramshackle house and tattered appearance attested that her money went elsewhere. Drink—that all too common vice—held a siren-like call over her. Each day, Trudy would gather her earnings and each night, she would exchange a large portion of them for a shot at happiness. She never found it.

Trudy's misery was exceeded only by that of her son. He has had many names throughout his life, but for the sake of this narrative, we will assume that his name was Frayne, meaning 'stranger'. It is close enough to the truth. Upon first beholding her son, Trudy announced, "He's a stranger to me, just like his father." She seemed incapable of accepting him as her own, and in return, Frayne held no love for her.

The circumstances surrounding Frayne's birth were not uncommon. His father was a traveller passing through, a stranger in every town he visited, and Trudy was just another drunken woman in a pub. Nine months after they met, Frayne was born.

Some days I almost find myself pitying Trudy. She neither wanted nor expected a child. But then I remember how her displeasure was painted in blue and fading yellow bruises upon Frayne's skin, and I cannot forgive her.

What must it do to a child to be brought up like this? You see such children everywhere on the streets of our cities. They are poor, filthy wretches who are flayed and abused both in body and soul until a scab knits itself over their hearts to stop the bleeding. What is more important to a child than a mother's love? If it is not given, they must either search for it elsewhere or harden their hearts to all feelings.

There, Mr Simmons, those were my broad strokes. The scene is set, and I shall now begin my story in earnest.

CHAPTER TWO

It had rained the night before. The cobbles were still slick, and the air held the damp smell of passing rainfall that did nothing to mask the stench of fish. Trudy's voice, mingling with the cacophony of peddler's cries, seemed to be the only one that reached Frayne's ears. "Fish! Come and get your bleeding fish! Fresh as you like, cheap as you like! Filthy brat, keep your hands off! Fish!"

Frayne was six and forced to endure his days by the quayside watching Trudy haggle over her slimy wares. He wouldn't learn her trade—why should he bother? He knew he would never sell fish. The year before, when he was five years old and, to his mind, still quite a baby, he dreamed of being a great warrior or a wealthy noble. He had heard many stories of such men at the pub, and a life of war or wealth seemed terribly exciting. However, now he was six, he knew he would be a traveller, just like the father he had never met. Wherever he went, he would be a stranger, no one would know where he came from or who his mother was. In the eyes of a passerby, he could be a knight or a king in disguise. To him, that was freedom. For all Frayne considered himself worldly-wise, he was still just a child with a dream born out of his shame.

On that damp day, something else was introduced into his life. Bored and tired, Frayne crouched on the cobblestones, scratching pictures onto their weathered surface with a piece of slate. Curiously, he watched as a boy darted out from behind a corner, collided with a passerby, and then hurried away in Frayne's direction. The boy stopped, and Frayne heard the tell-tale chink of coins in his palm.

"Wot you do that for?" Frayne called out.

The boy started, then, seeing the size and nature of his audience, merely grinned and with a swagger replied, "Rich toff. What's he gonna miss a few coppers?"

I'm sure that the "toff" in question was far from being well off, but to a young boy with hardly a farthing to his name, well, wealth is all a matter of perspective.

"How d'you do it?" Frayne asked him.

The boy grinned again, pleased with the attention. "Bump him and grab his purse. 'S not hard, watch." So saying, he collided with Frayne, and though he was prepared for it, Frayne did not feel the small hand reach into his pocket and draw out the filthy rag that was its sole contents. "See? It's a lark!" And with a laugh, the boy ran off jingling his coins and waving Frayne's handkerchief in the air.

This encounter opened a world of possibility for Frayne. He was unfamiliar with the meaning of the word "full" in relation to food, and shoes were luxuries that featured only in the lives of others. Simply put, he was poor, young, and desperate, and after all, who among the passers-by on the quayside would miss a few shillings? As soon as the boy was out of sight, Frayne rose to his feet to try his luck. His first attempt ended with a clout on the ear, the second with a bloody nose.

As all children find, practice increases prowess, and the more he practised, the more adept Frayne became in the illicit art of pickpocketing. It seemed that he possessed a gift, unethical though it was, for taking that which did not belong to him. Every penny he took sent a thrill through him. He could have been rich, and still, he would have stolen for the sheer rush and satisfaction it brought him.

Frayne had not given up his dream of travelling, and his newfound talent added another dimension to his ambition. If he was to be a stranger, why be a poor one? At the very least, he could maintain the appearance of affluence. He kept his money hidden beneath his mattress, out of sight of Trudy, and over time it grew to a sum that seemed immense to a boy of such limited means.

The problem with thrills, sadly, is their tendency to become mundane as time passes. As the ease of the action increases, the satisfaction inevitably dissipates until one finds oneself pushing the bounds of one's capabilities to maintain the thrill that makes the risk worth taking. It was precisely this that came to afflict Frayne. After a couple of years, small coins and trinkets no longer held the same interest for him. So it was that one day, he returned home from the quay, not with his usual little allotment of coins but with a gentleman's watch in his pocket.

Gentlemen were rare commodities in Frayne's experience, only ever appearing at the quay if they had business to conduct or had become lost. The watch was the most beautiful object Frayne had beheld in his short eight years of life. It was pale-faced, edged in gold-coloured metal, and inscribed with ebony markings. Frayne found he could not risk damaging it by adding it to the collection under his mattress, but there were few hiding places in that small house. When Trudy arrived home early—staggeringly drunk and ill-tempered—she was in time to witness her son prying up a kitchen floorboard.

Anger and fear motivated her that night. The anger was ever-present, and the fear came from knowing what would fall upon her should her son's actions be discovered. Frayne knew only terror and pain. He was used to Trudy's drunken rages, but never had he experienced such a torrent of abuse. His whole body became her canvas, the bright red that streamed from his nose adding vibrancy to the mottled blues and purples that were already painting themselves onto the paleness of his skin. That night ended in darkness and a child's bleeding heart.

The darkness eventually resolved itself into a paler blackness, then a fading grey as Frayne's consciousness returned. Pain paralyzed him until fear leant movement to his limbs, postponing the stiffness and urging him up from the floor to his mattress and out of the door, clutching his money in one hand and the cursed watch in the other while Trudy still lay prone upon her bed in a drunken stupor.

CHAPTER THREE

There was every chance that Frayne's frantic escape would end in disaster. Without heeding direction, he made his way to a larger town five miles from his home, where all too frequently one could see small, dirty figures lying in the gutters, bruises blossoming on their faces and their belongings vanished; testaments to the cruelty that lives in us all. Fortunately for Frayne, and indeed, many others who would know him later, when he finally collapsed, it was not in a gutter but on a doorstep.

The owner of the doorstep was a lady by the name of Mrs Alves. Mrs Alves was fortunate enough to reside in the better part of the town. She was not a wealthy woman but remembered a time when her state of living had been greatly improved. Her husband had been a merchant—and a fairly successful one at that—before he had died from consumption, leaving his wife and young daughter in fear of contagion themselves.

After his death, most of Mr Alves' remaining assets had fallen to his creditors, leaving only a small portion for his family. Grieved though she was by her husband's death,

Mrs Alves was not one to become distracted by misery. Her daughter was her life and must be sustained, so within days, Mrs Alves had found work at a small bakery.

The easiest course of action after her husband's death, of course, would have been to remarry. Barely into her thirties, Mrs Alves had lost none of her youthful beauty, but she was a faithful soul and was loathe to abandon her husband's memory so soon after his departure. Mrs Alves did not consider the work at the bakery to be beneath her; she had grown up in a poorer family, only to find herself happily elevated in station when her husband's business succeeded far beyond their imagination. Her life with Mr Alves had been a bright spot of light in her existence that, as all lights eventually do, went out. Her main concern was that she would be unable to support her daughter. However, she need not have worried—her diligence and charm saw her promoted within the bakery until she found herself quite comfortable in her means.

It was late when Mrs Alves discovered the urchin on her doorstep. The night was held back by the glow of lamps hanging outside each house, casting pale pools of light onto the ground. The lanterns may have diminished the darkness, but they did nothing to mitigate the cold, and it was with reluctance that Mrs Alves opened her door to her cat. She did not immediately notice Frayne, wrapped in the darkness as he was, but as she turned back to the warmth of her home, the light from within caught the huddled mass, and she paused. She opened the door more fully, but even with the added light, she would not have identified the lump as a child were it not for the small, pale hand that extended from it.

Frayne was huddled into a grimy shirt; dark, matted hair covered his face, and the limbs that were visible were disguised by layers of mud and dried blood. It was a pitiful sight and one that caught Mrs Alves' heart. Gingerly, she gathered him into her arms, barely feeling his weight. Once inside, it became clear just how desperate the boy's situation was. His face, beneath the signs of abuse, was as pale as the moon, and his breath came in faint, rattling gasps. Mrs Alves paused, her breath catching in her throat. Had the consumption that had taken her husband from her now returned to her home in the form of this wraith? But she could not, would not leave the child to die; his shrunken form seemed to be barely that of a five-year-old. What if it was her daughter in his place, wouldn't she want someone to care for her? The boy would stay, and she prayed for God to restore his life and protect them all.

Frayne awoke to a sombre face peering down at him. For a moment it reminded him of his watch—pale and framed with gold, but the eyes were dusty green, not ebony. He looked frantically around for the watch and saw it resting on a small table just out of his reach. He glanced back at the face above him—it looked amused now. He opened his mouth to speak, but no sound emerged.

"Here." the face said and handed him a mug whose contents he readily swallowed. Frayne looked back and saw that the face belonged to a little girl who sat on a coarse wooden chair beside his bed. She grinned at him. "What's your name?"

"Frayne." his voice came out as little more than a gasp. How long had he been unconscious?

"Fray? Who calls their child Fray?"

Was the expression on her face one of derision or curiosity he wondered. "FrayNE. It means 'stranger'." His voice came more easily now, but the girl seemed unimpressed, "What's yours?"

“I’m Farrah," she responded with a flick of her head, "it means beautiful."

Frayne gave a harsh laugh, "Was your mother blind?" Why he responded that way, he did not understand. Truthfully, he thought her name very apt, but something in him was broken and hurt, and he could not bear to let anyone near him for fear of deepening that pain.

Farrah’s eyes narrowed, and she looked ready to fly at him. Mrs Alves arrived in the sickroom just as her daughter’s mouth was opening, a scathing retort fresh upon her tongue. Mrs Alves was all too familiar with her daughter’s hot temper, and she hurried the little girl away with a warning look that barely covered the laughter that was bubbling up within her.

Mrs Alves eyed Frayne critically, then sat beside him on the bed and began spooning hot soup down his throat. "Well, you don't have the consumption, so your lungs are safe, but as for the rest of you…" she trailed off. Frayne merely watched her with wide-eyed fascination. In his entire eight years of life, he had never seen a woman like her—clean, well-kept, and beautiful, with a voice that sounded like it had never spoken a harsh word before.

When Frayne had finished the soup, Mrs Alves reached out towards his forehead, but he instinctively coiled backwards from her outstretched hand. She paused, and her gaze softened somewhat, "I'm afraid you've been very ill." She addressed him as though he were a wild animal she hoped to tame, "Your body is weak and will take a long time to recover. For the present, I would advise you to remain here until your strength returns. That is if you would like to?"

Frayne nodded dumbly. Something about the tone of her voice and the heavy feeling of the soup resting in his stomach lulled him. Quite against his will, he felt his eyes growing heavy again, and with a sigh, he surrendered to his exhaustion. When Farrah returned to Frayne's room, her temper quickly forgotten, she found her mother sitting on the bed, cradling the inert boy's head in her lap.

From that moment forward, Frayne felt that he had a true home. As far as he was concerned, Trudy was no parent to him, Mrs Alves was now his mother, and Farrah was his best friend. Although Frayne had found people to love, the change within himself was slow in coming. The wounds left by childhood trauma rarely heal fully, and Frayne's heart was badly scarred. He was skittish, stubborn, and at times, belligerent. His coarse language and behaviour initially shocked Farrah, who had, up until his arrival, led a moderately sheltered life. Nightmares tormented his sleep, and he would often wake crying, but each time, Mrs Alves was there to hold and comfort him. He loved her with a fierceness that only those who have never known love before can possess, and in return, she loved him as tenderly as any true mother can love her son.

As for Farrah, she loved him too. Though she adored her mother, she had often found herself lonely with no siblings and few friends to pass the time with. Once she became accustomed to her mother's strange charge, she realised she could not have asked for a better friend. Her lighthearted confidence and wild abandon drew him out of himself, and she made him laugh—a rare gift to one as damaged as he. His temper was not as quick as hers, and he had a calming, steadying influence on her, much to Mrs Alves' relief.

Frayne told Farrah of his dream to travel and delighted her with exaggerated tales of his exploits at the quay. Besides those stories, he never spoke of anything else about his life before he met them, and they never enquired. I believe that Mrs Alves guessed much of his history, but

Farrah was content in her innocence, and Mrs Alves saw no need to disturb that. As Frayne immersed himself in his new life, he found himself forgetting Trudy more and more. It was as if a door in his mind was closing, finally shutting away the pain of the past.

After two months with Mrs Alves and Farrah, Frayne began his education. Mrs Alves had been trying to replicate a recipe she had learned at the bakery, and Farrah and Frayne had been sitting near her, telling each other wild tales of adventure.

"Farrah darling, would you read this for me?" Mrs Alves asked, passing her daughter a wadded sheet of paper.

Frayne listened in astonishment as the obscure black markings on the page were brought to life by Farrah's voice.

Feeling his stare and anticipating criticism, Farrah paused and glared at him, "Yes?"

"What are you doing?"

"Have you never seen someone read before?"

"Well, I..." he was loathe to admit his ignorance.

"Oh." Sensing his embarrassment, Farrah softened, "Well, you see, the words we speak are made up of sounds, but sounds don't stick to paper, so each sound has a letter we can write down. That way, when someone else sees the letter, they can read the sounds and know the words." She glanced over at her mother, a hint of pride upon her face. Her recitation was carefully given and had taken much prior thought.

Mrs Alves nodded and smiled at her son, "Perhaps we can teach you." she ventured, "I will make a gentleman out of you yet, and between us, perhaps we can make a lady out of Farrah." She swatted playfully at her daughter who was at that moment, dipping her fingers into the mixing bowl.

Mrs Alves did seem determined to transform Frayne into a gentleman. As well as reading and writing, she incorporated poetry and music into his education. Farrah took it upon herself to instruct him in the arts of dancing and drawing, and in return, he taught her how to swim.

Both Frayne's speech and manner gained refinement, and properly dressed, any observer would have been hard-pressed to identify him as anything less than a little cavalier. It seemed that Frayne was a seed that needed only love to grow. He was highly intelligent, that much was readily apparent, but he also possessed a unique creativity that amazed Mrs Alves. He came to appreciate beauty and delighted in surprising his new family with gifts.

He returned home one day from a foray to the edges of town with two bright bunches of wildflowers clutched in his hands. He presented one to Farrah with pride and the other to his mother with a kiss. In those days, he laughed easily and often, and Mrs Alves felt that a bright light had come to her home to chase away the shadows left by her husband's death.

Over time, Frayne's nightmares subsided, but now and again, something hiding deep within the recesses of his mind would creep forward into his dreams. He awoke one night in the darkness, confused and panicked, with a fleeting feeling of loneliness and pain. Turning his head towards the door, he saw Mrs Alves entering, carrying a small candle. Gently, she set it down beside him, and he watched as its pale flickering light seemed to dare the darkness to encroach.

"Frayne." She murmured, gathering him into her arms, smoothing his hair as if to brush away the lingering dreams. She held him until she thought he was asleep again. As she moved to lay him down, he stirred.

"Do you love me?" He asked. The question seemed to creep from his lips, then shrink before her, small and pitiful, fearful and ashamed.

She held him even tighter, "My sweet, you bring me so much joy. You are my dearly loved son, and I shall never let you go, my Frayne."

That was all he needed to hear, all that he had ever wanted to hear. He fell asleep with a smile on his face and a healing heart.

This next part nearly breaks me to write, so I shall not dwell upon it. Four years after Mrs Alves first discovered Frayne on her doorstep, she fell ill. It was the kind of illness that could only end in one manner. Barely conscious, she fought the encroaching darkness for the sake of her children, the most precious things in the world to her, but after three days, life bid her farewell, death took her by the hand, and together they departed.

To Frayne and Farrah, it felt as though a part of themselves had departed with her. They had watched the shadow of death steal across their mother's face and were present at the moment her light vanished from their lives forever. For a time, the two children lived in a kind of limbo, suspended in grief, unaware of anything around them, conscious only of the gaping hole that had been opened in their hearts by death's cruel fingers.

Frayne found himself motherless once again. The wounds that Trudy had inflicted upon his heart re-opened, though they had been so close to healing. The light had gone from his life, and he was awash in grief and aching and anger. This time, however, he was not alone—Farrah shared in his anguish, and through the days following Mrs

Alves' death, their grief knit them closer together. They retired from the world to the top floor of their house, where they sat locked in an embrace—two children sharing their past joys and their present heartache. They were unaware of the passing of time. Their worlds darkened, and they slept only when their sorrow proved too heavy to bear.

Life did not permit Frayne and Farrah to grieve for long. Even today, orphans are considered something of a pest. Pests must be dealt with—put in their proper place—lest they spread and overwhelm a town, consuming its food, spreading filth, and harassing its inhabitants. We are cruel to think this way. Farrah, sheltered by her mother's love, was oblivious to this mindset, but Frayne was all too aware of it.

Farrah was the first to break the silence that had enveloped them since their mother's death. "Frayne, what will happen to us?" Her voice was hollow and uncaring, as though the future they faced no longer mattered.

"I suppose we will be taken to the workhouse." Frayne's reply was equally hollow.

Farrah stirred, "Perhaps not. A kind neighbour might care for us, or someone from the bakery, or we might go to a nice orphanage, or perhaps…perhaps you have family that will have us?"

Poor, desperate, ignorant Farrah. She could not imagine a world in which no one would take pity on a motherless child.

"No, we will be taken to the workhouse." Frayne's voice was not as empty as before—the mention of his family had stirred up the anger that was resting within him.

"Is it so impossible that anyone could want us?" Farrah's usually strong voice was close to breaking.

"Yes."

"No, you are wrong, our mother wanted us. Do you think she would just leave us if she thought we would end up alone?"

"Our mother is dead, Farrah! She is dead! She does not care what happens to us now!" His pain and anger broke free and hit her like a blow.

She recoiled from him, "I hate you, Frayne." Her whisper cut itself into his heart. A miserable silence stretched out over them.

Frayne tentatively reached towards her, "Farrah, I'm sorry." It seemed so pitiful, so insignificant, but he was hurting too. "You are not alone, you have me." What consolation was that he wondered. "We don't have to go to the workhouse, we can run away. It will be an adventure, just you and I." an old excitement flared within him.

"But where will we live? Where will we find the money for food?"

"We will live in the city, of course, and we will steal what we need. Think about it, everyone in the city is wealthy! I used to think, 'What would people miss a few farthings?', but in the city, people wouldn't miss any number of shillings, maybe even pounds!" his eyes were shining now with the thrill of a boyish dream, "We could be rich Farrah! And you could be a Lady, just like Mother wanted. Imagine, you could wear pearls and silk dresses and rings on every finger…" he trailed off at the expression on her face. It was not the excitement he had expected but sorrow and bitter disappointment.

"No, Frayne."

The cut that her whisper had opened inside of him moments before cracked, and he thought his heart well and truly broken. "Why?" The fleeting flash of joy was gone.

"Stealing? That is not what Mother would have wanted."

"I cannot go to the workhouse." His voice was flat. Fear

was creeping in now, and he wanted only to escape.

She nodded. That was the answer that she had expected. "Then I will go so you will know where to find me."

Frayne did not protest, though perhaps he should have. Unlike Farrah, he knew what such places were like, but his grief had settled back upon him as heavy as a mountain, and he could not speak. I ask you, Mr Simmons, not to judge Frayne too harshly.

When the men came to take them to the workhouse, they found only one child. A small wraith of a girl waited for them, her face ringed in gold, her heart bleeding in her chest, and a small pocket watch ticking in her hands.

CHAPTER FOUR

Once again Frayne was running, this time with empty hands, but with a destination that held promise. In his mind, the city was a fantastic place full of hope and adventure. He had heard tales of it on the quayside—an unfathomably large gathering of buildings, cobbled roads, houses, shops, and stalls. It was the home of the wealthy and the only destination for a person seeking adventure and fortune.

The journey passed in a bittersweet haze of excitement and grief. Imaginings of glorious escapades wove through his mind and tangled around the more recent memories of Farrah crying as she held him close, then waving goodbye as he left. Although it hurt to admit it, even to himself, Frayne knew that he would never see her again. Farrah was ill-prepared for the cruel life that now faced her, and even if she escaped the workhouse, Frayne knew she would not look for him. She had entered his life for a season, and as summer darkens into autumn, then winter, that season had ended.

Frayne walked alone the first day, then travelled with a band of pilgrims for the next two. He reached the city on the fourth day, his grieving complete—or so he told himself. The acute pain that his mother's death had evoked within him had faded into a dull ache at the prospect of a new life. As for his memories of Trudy and the wounds bound up with them, he believed them to be gone, washed away by the thrill of the city. In truth, hurt and alone with no one to console him, Frayne had buried his grief and anguish deep within himself where he need not face it.

That first morning he wandered the city streets in an awed daze. People thronged the thoroughfares, and horses and carts raced by, threatening to crush him. The air was heavy with the scent of vendors' wares, dust, and more personal smells, which all mixed with the cacophony of human voices, creating a heady atmosphere. From a distance, Frayne saw a Lady dressed all in silks, riding a fine horse, and for a moment he thought her face was Farrah's.

The day passed in a whirlwind of ecstasy, and it was with exhausted relief that he finally lay down in a doorway to sleep. The cold and discomfort seemed to greet him with an old familiarity that was not completely unwelcome to Frayne. When darkness wrapped its inky shroud around the city, he was too deep asleep to hear the sound of approaching footsteps, the whisper of knives being drawn, and the low, animal noise of a hunter spotting its prey.

Rough hands jerked him awake, dragging him from the confines of the doorway and lifting him until his feet no longer touched the ground.

"What we want," a low voice growled, "is your money or your life."

A coarse laugh erupted from behind the form that held Frayne. Blinking back the fog clinging to his eyes, he could make out two figures. The first, still holding Frayne up by his shirt, seemed a veritable giant. His hair hung over his face, obscuring much but leaving his feral eyes free. His clothes were tattered and faded, and he exuded the strong smell of alcohol. His companion was as wiry as he was thick, with hooded eyes that held a hungry glint. Neither of the two could have been any older than fourteen.

Frayne's mind raced, "Good evening, Gentlemen. I am afraid you have caught me at my worst."

The boy who held him paused, a sneer creeping over his face, and his companion laughed again, "It seems we've found ourselves a right toff." he spat the last two words, "What're you doing here?"

"Sleeping, you tosspot." And with a curse that would have made Farrah blush, Frayne kicked out hard in the direction of his assailant's crotch.

The boy had been expecting such a move and thrust his hips backwards while at the same time shifting his grip on Frayne and swinging his fist towards his face in a remarkable display of coordination. The blow connected with a force that painted stars before Frayne's eyes and left him lying disoriented on the ground, a bruise blossoming on his cheek and the smell of alcohol surrounding him.

In a daze, Frayne thought that he saw Trudy's face looming above him, her foot drawn back to kick, but it was his mugger's face, awash with surprise, that collapsed onto the cobblestones beside him. Frayne gazed uncomprehendingly at the lifeless figure next to him, then startled as a loud, shrieking cry stabbed at his ears. It came again as he struggled to rise, an unholy screech that made him pause. Slowly, his eyes regained their focus, and Frayne found himself gaping at the sight of a small boy cavorting around the prone body of the wiry thug—shrieking, whooping, and hurling curses at its uncomprehending ears. The boy finally spat on his victim and then, seemingly satisfied, made his way over to Frayne, pausing to spit on the second body.

"Who're you?" the boy demanded.

Frayne stammered out his name. The ground was spinning now, and his face hurt—why did his face hurt?

"Frayne?" The boy looked at him closely, "Trudy's Frayne?" Then he laughed, "We all thought she'd offed you and hid the body. Bound to off someone, complete blazing loon that she is. No offense to your good self mind you." He spat on the senseless thug again for good measure and squinted good-naturedly at Frayne.

"You killed him." Frayne could feel a cold shock creeping into his limbs. Was he hallucinating?

"Nah, just knocked him out. Not sure I can say the same for the other one though." he squinted back to where the wiry boy lay with a dark trickle pooling by his head. "Can't say they didn't deserve it, those blithering idiots."

"I am not Trudy's. She is not my mother." fragments of the boy's previous statements were settling into Frayne's mind.

"Well, whatever she is, 'She bears a duke's revenues on her back, and in her heart she scorns our poverty'."

"What?" Frayne's thoughts were swirling in a senseless mass which matched the spinning ground.

The boy rubbed his nose on his wrist, "'S poetry."

"Oh," A distant memory slunk from the mist surrounding Frayne's thoughts to the forefront of his mind, "'Shall I not live to be avenged on her? Contemptuous base-born callout as she is…' William Shakespeare. But what has that to do with Trudy?"

The boy seemed impressed by his knowledge, "You've had a right proper education then. Good on you. Don't matter what poetry has to do with it, the muse descended upon me and there was now't I could do but speak."

"The muse descended upon Shakespeare." Slowly the fog began to release its grip on Frayne's mind.

"Well, now it's descended on me. Right, let's go."

"What?"

"'Defer no time, delays have dangerous ends.'"

"More Shakespeare?" Frayne asked weakly. He was beginning to wonder if he had gone mad or if he really was speaking to some crazed phantom of the night. Darkness, deeper than that of the sky, was now rimming Frayne's vision.

"Right good man was Shakespeare, wrote some nice poesy. I'll be like him someday, got meself a talent for verse I have, but for now, let's go before someone with a bigger brick gets here." Frayne looked down and saw that the boy had indeed used a brick to incapacitate his two assailants.

"Who are you?" Frayne allowed a demanding edge to creep into his voice in a vain attempt to appear authoritative—an air belied by the fact that he was still crouched on the cobblestones, unable to rise.

"You don't recognise me?" The boy's tone was one of laughing disbelief. He strode backwards into the light of a building, struck a pose worthy of a Grecian statue, and, spreading his hands, declared, "'I am that merry wanderer of the night', I am Adam."

The light cast itself in patches on Adam's face, and Frayne remembered, years ago, watching this same figure dart out from behind a corner and collide with a passerby. He could almost hear the rattle of coins in a small hand and Adam's voice declaring, "Rich toff. What's he gonna miss a few coppers?". There was no poetry then, just nimble fingers and a theatrical swagger that still remained.

"You worked the quay as well," Frayne stated.

"Yeah, then moved onto summat better when the

stinking filth became unbearable. Not that there's less stinking filth here, but it's a different class of filth if you know what I mean." Adam grinned and winked at Frayne, "Right, I've decided I like you. We're from the same reeking hovel, you speak Shakespeare, and from what I remember, you ain't half bad at picking pockets neither." The wink came again, "Trust me, Mate, you won't survive one night here without help, and out of all of the thieving rats here, I'm the best rat you've got." He hauled Frayne to his feet and, partially supporting his weight, began staggering away from the two shadows slumped upon the cobbles. "Besides, you'll get yourself killed, or worse sleeping in doorways. I know somewhere better."

That 'somewhere better' was a rooftop, far above the tangled mass of streets below. The two figures huddled against a cooling chimney, grateful for the last vestiges of warmth it provided.

"What I cannot comprehend," Frayne spoke slowly, exhaustion lending weight to his tongue, "is why one moment you speak as though you are a great orator onstage, and the next, like a beggar in the pits."

"'For I have neither wit nor words nor worth, action nor utterance nor the power of speech, to stir men's blood.'" Adam murmured, "What I cannot comprehend," he pronounced the words slowly, "is why Trudy's son talks like the King himself."

"I told you, I am not Trudy's son."

"Suit yourself," Adam replied and promptly fell asleep.

Each of us has a means of soothing the wounds in our hearts—Adam's balm was words. His childhood was spent in the cruellest of worlds, one hardly visible to us fortunate few who pass through it unawares. The streets are our largest orphanages, where children find that the alleyways become their beds, the gutters their graves. They are hurt and hunted by those driven to desperation or by the watchmen, sworn to protect others from the disease, the contamination that is these broken souls. Their bodies are painted in the darkest shades, and their hearts are coloured likewise until they become the monsters they fear.

Starvation haunts them, and sickness seizes them—there is no hope for these wretched souls. All too often, their 'balm' becomes violence and crime as they seek to lose their pain in ruthlessness. Curiously, Adam found his respite in the beauty of poetry. Where in his coarse world he discovered Shakespeare, I shall never know, but the words moved him. He knew of no beauty of his own, so he borrowed some and committed it to memory, making it a part of himself—the part that soothed and healed and gave him hope that his misery would not last forever.

The watery light of morning roused Adam and dispelled the shadows that obscured his face. Frayne's image of a phantom the night before seemed to be confirmed by the daylight. The boy was a ghost, pale-skinned beneath the dirt that covered him, fair-haired, and with a face made angular by hunger—insignificant and forgettable until he opened his eyes. They were the colour of freezing water, and full of a feral intensity but behind the ferocity was a calculated shrewdness that made his gaze unforgettable. It was his smile though, that changed his visage from one of animal ferocity or ghostly transparency to one of impish mischief. Observing him, Frayne could easily believe that Adam was no mortal boy but a faery, perhaps even Puck himself, sprung from the mind he so clearly revered.

If Adam was pale light, Frayne was all darkness. His hair

was black, just black, and hung in unkempt curtains over his forehead. Two inky wells, full of pain, gazed out from a face which, like Adam's, was angular, though not from a lack of food. No smile lightened his countenance. What a pair they must have made that morning, crouched upon the roof—an imp and his demon.

"Right, I'm hungry, let's go," Adam said as soon as he opened his eyes.

Together, he and Frayne began to descend from the rooftop, Adam leaping and darting across the slates with wild abandon, swinging himself down, and finally dropping to the pavement below. Frayne watched him with curious fascination. He could not recall ascending to the chimney the previous night and was unsure how he had managed it in his dazed state.

Frayne had always considered himself nimble, but compared to Adam, he felt clumsy and unwieldy. Nevertheless, Frayne followed him with all the grace and agility he could muster—badly scraping his leg in the process—and landed square upon his feet at the bottom. He fixed Adam with a sure stare as though daring him to remark, but the boy seemed not to have noticed his struggle and continued down the alleyway into which they had descended.

The hushed feeling that had settled upon Frayne since he awoke shattered the moment he emerged onto the street. Once again, he was almost bowled over by a farmer's cart as he gazed around in bewilderment at the masses of people already swarming in the streets. Adam, seemingly unperturbed, began making his way through the throng, ducking and weaving until Frayne was forced into a run to keep pace with him. They paused across the street from a vendor's cart.

"Right, rules," Adam stated with an air of poorly concealed excitement. "First off, anything you've heard about the city, toss it, it's shite. This ain't some gentleman's paradise, 'Hell is empty and all the devils are here.' So say, 'Adam, I know now't about the city.'"

Frayne stared solemnly back at him, "Adam, I know nothing about the city."

A crease appeared on Adam's forehead, "No, 'Adam, I know now't about the city.' You act like a gentleman, you get treated like a gentleman and find yourself in the gutter with a red smile on your throat and no purse."

"I don't have a purse."

"Say it."

"Adam, I know now't about the city."

"Good, now rules. Stay away from alleys."

"What about the one we just came out of?"

"Shut up, lemme finish. Stay away from alleys unless you're with me. Don't run 'round when it's dark unless you're with me. Don't try to rob dockworkers or those." Here he pointed to a short thin man, with a pale face, and dark circles ringing his vacant-looking eyes.

"Why?" Frayne asked curiously.

"'Cause I said. And lastly, never rob the same man twice. So, that brings us here. That," he pointed towards the vendor's cart, "is breakfast. Go get it." So saying, he pushed Frayne into the stream of humanity and leaned back to watch.

Frayne felt only a moment of panic before the thrill of anticipation gripped him. He ran through the crowd, weaving between passersby—nimble and eager, until he collided head-on with a man turning away from the vendor's stall, a freshly baked pie in his hand.

"Shove off!"

Frayne was elbowed rudely backwards, and he stumbled, landing in an embarrassed heap upon the cobbles. "Sorry," he murmured breathlessly, his face flushing red as he scrambled to his feet. "Sorry." He muttered again as he turned to face the vendor, "One pie, please."

The man squinted at him but handed him the pie without complaint as Frayne meticulously counted out three coins from his palm.

"Thank you." Frayne reached out a hand to take the pie, then hurried back across the road to where Adam waited for his return. "Here." Frayne handed him the pie, a touch of pride colouring his voice.

Adam sniffed it, "You should've got two."

"One was easier, less risky."

"You're more obvious than you used to be, taking the purse off that man you ran into. You're lucky he didn't notice."

"It's been a while since I've practised."

"Hm, you should've just taken the pies. Don't spend money to eat."

Frayne grinned and produced the three coins he had handed to the vendor. Adam gaped for a moment before mirroring Frayne's grin.

"I took the coins off him when I took the pie."

Adam laughed and glanced at him with a new appreciation, "Breakfast and money? 'Not Trudy's Son' has brains! Wish I'd thought of that meself." He playfully jostled Frayne and handed him half the pie, "'Fair thoughts and happy hours attend on you!'"

So they continued together. For Frayne, thievery was a sport. It kept him alive, but it was a game nevertheless. He delighted in concocting elaborate plots that gave him the thrill he considered an almost greater necessity for his existence than money. The two were something of an enigma. Whereas Adam was all laughter and wild abandon, Frayne held a calm, steady air about himself. Yet when it came to larceny, Frayne displayed an uninhibited delight in stark contrast to Adam's more practical approach.

To begin with, Adam was bewildered by the creature he had taken in. But in time, the boy's sheer enthusiasm beguiled him, and he found himself giving in to Frayne's daring plans with an avid readiness. One thing, however, persisted in disconcerting Adam. He knew Frayne as Trudy's son—a bright, enthusiastic, common boy with an unfortunate mother. The educated, self-assured child was quite an alteration, but as the streets slowly wore away at Frayne's debonair manners and appearance, a different, darker creature was in part revealed. It was this darkness that unnerved Adam. It was not readily apparent but flitted like a shadow deep beneath Frayne's surface, infrequently visible even to him. He often wondered whether Frayne knew that within himself, beneath the exuberant, amiable exterior lurked a devil.

CHAPTER FIVE

"What d' you know about chimneys?" Frayne asked one morning.

Adam gave him a blank stare, "Chimneys? They let out smoke, stop a house burning down, make nice warm places to sleep…" Adam trailed off, "What now? Either you think I'm an idiot, or you've got some stupid plan in your head that's gonna get me hurt again. I swear, 'I am a man more sinned against than sinning.'" He rubbed angrily at his shoulder which bore a large bruise. "If this has anything to do with that shoemaker's house…"

"It's got nothing to do with the shoemaker's house…"

"Fine plan of yours that was! 'We'll break in through the window at night, Adam. There'll be no one there at night, Adam.'"

"It would've worked if you hadn't been so bleeding loud."

"Loud? I wasn't the one who smashed the window with a rock instead of prying it open."

Frayne coloured, "I thought he'd be asleep by then."

"Clearly, shoemakers stay up all night in their workrooms.

God knows why."

Frayne grinned, "You should've seen the look on his face…"

"Well, I couldn't, could I? Too busy getting hit by his hammer."

"Who knew a shoemaker could throw so well?"

Adam scowled again, "If you think I'm going to climb down his chimney in the middle of the night, you're dead wrong."

Frayne's eyes lit up, "So people can climb up and down chimneys?"

"Course they can. Haven't you seen the little beggars with their brushes popping up and down them? Scared the life out of me first time I saw it. Popped up right next to me and almost knocked me off the roof. I'm not going down the shoemaker's chimney."

"No one's going down the shoemaker's chimney. I was thinking of a bigger one, a gentleman's chimney."

Adam stared at him in disbelief, "You want to go down a gentleman's chimney? For what?"

"Money, clothes, watches, whatever I can find."

"So, you'll just pop down, take whatever's there, and pray that no one's around to see you?"

"Yes." Frayne grinned again, "It'll be fun."

"That's what you said about robbing the shoemaker."

"Enough with your bleeding shoemaker. Come on, Adam, just one time?"

It was not long before they found a suitable chimney. The gentleman to whom it belonged was in town on business and rarely at home. Though his staff was small, the plan was still reckless, and both Frayne and Adam knew it. There wasn't much joy in their lives, and what little there was, they created themselves. Reckless plans brought adventure, and adventure brought joy–or at least a thrill of anticipation which could be considered joy. If all went wrong, they both knew that their lives could not be much worse than they already were and perhaps this knowledge made them careless. They had each other, and little else mattered. They would live together, and they would die together, whether from starvation, accident, or the gallows they did not much care.

Crouching next to the gentleman's chimney, Adam looked seriously at Frayne, "We should've got a rope before trying this."

Frayne smiled easily, "We don't have a rope, and I don't need one. I'll climb down, listen for anyone in the room, and if no one's there, I'll pick up some small things and climb straight back up."

"If there's anyone in the room, they'll hear you coming down."

"I'll be quiet."

"No, you won't."

"I will, and I'll be careful. Just think of what we'll get if this works."

"I'm thinking of what we'll get if it doesn't."

"We've done worse things. Just watch the street and call down the chimney if anyone comes near the house."

Adam nodded, then anxiously watched as Frayne climbed atop the chimney and with a great deal of scuffling, squeezed himself down it. Even from the roof's edge where he lay watching the street, Adam could hear faint rustles as Frayne worked his way down the chimney.

After what seemed an age, an eerily distorted whisper floated up to the rooftop, "I made it. No one's here."

"Well, hurry up then." Adam hissed back down.

The words, "Filthy chimney…dust everywhere." floated

up to him.

After about fifteen minutes, Adam heard faint scraping noises from the chimney again, and Frayne called out that he was coming back up. Satisfied, Adam returned to the edge of the roof for a last glance at the street, just in time to see the master of the house stepping through the doorway below.

He rushed to the chimney and called as loudly as he dared, "The master's here. Hurry up."

More noise from the chimney followed this statement, and then it stopped. "Adam, I'm stuck."

Adam could feel the blood draining from his face, "Well, get unstuck and move faster."

"Someone's coming."

Adam waited, afraid to move, almost afraid to breathe, as if he were the one trapped in the narrow chimney awaiting discovery. Each minute passed with unbearable slowness, and he felt as if he was a part of some strange dream. Any moment now, he would wake up, laugh, and tell Frayne that he had dreamed they were climbing down chimneys in search of treasure. Only he wouldn't tell Frayne because Frayne would probably think it was a wonderful idea, and he would have to endure this bizarre situation all over again.

The minutes turned into hours, and Adam worried and waited as he watched the sun slip beneath the skyline and the moon rise above the buildings. There had been no further sounds from the chimney, and Adam didn't dare call down to Frayne lest the person in the room below should hear him. At long last, sounds of motion came from the chimney once more, and after twenty minutes, Adam could see Frayne's face peering up at him from the shaft.

"Give me a hand," Frayne whispered.

Adam reached down into the chimney as far as he could

go and grasped his friend's waiting hand. He pulled with every bit of his strength, and soon, Frayne was back on the rooftop once more.

"We should leave," Frayne said in a low voice, and together they hurried from the roof.

Once they had hidden at the back of a quiet alley, Adam stopped to examine his friend. Frayne was barely recognizable, dishevelled and covered in soot as he was, with blood running down his face, hands, and legs, and one arm hanging lower than the other. Relief and anger almost overwhelmed Adam. "What happened?" he demanded.

"It went well at first. The chimney was filthy, and soot kept falling as I climbed, so when I got to the bottom, the floor was covered. I was in a big room with books, and tables, and not much else. I cleaned the floor best I could, but it took a while, and by the time I finished, I didn't want to spend much longer there. Then you called, so I grabbed what I could and started back up the chimney, only I was in a hurry, and my arm got trapped, and I couldn't move. Then some people came in the room, and I knew if I moved, they'd hear me or see the soot coming down, so I stayed where I was until they left, then I got my arm free and climbed back up."

"You got your arm free by dislocating your shoulder," Adam said, frowning at Frayne's arm.

"I still made it back up, though."

"Hold still while I put it back in place."

A few minutes later, Adam sat back and studied Frayne, "Right, that's done. So, what d'you get?" Frayne smiled, and reaching into his clothing, he pulled out a leather-bound book. Adam stared at him incredulously, "That's it?"

"I got some handkerchiefs too."

"All of that for a book and some handkerchiefs?"

Frayne could feel his temper rising to match Adam's. "I told you there wasn't much else there. Should I have searched the whole house? Stopped by the kitchen and asked the servants to direct me to the silverware? Books like these are worth a lot, and no one's gonna miss it."

Adam scowled, "If that book doesn't fetch us some dinner, I'll pitch it into the river."

Frayne grinned, "I'll wager it'll fetch us dinner and breakfast, too."

Adam looked somewhat mollified, "Next time you steal a book, make sure you take a silver candlestick or some such thing as well."

"Fine, I'll keep my eyes open for candlesticks from now on. And next time, we should look for a clean chimney. Maybe watch the chimney sweeps for a few days and go in after them. That way we won't leave soot all over the floors."

Adam was alarmed, "Again? We're never doing that again, Mate. Promise me, no more chimneys."

Frayne looked belligerent for a moment, then, considering the bloodstains on his trousers and gingerly touching his shoulder, said, "Right, no more chimneys."

"And no more bleeding shoemakers. Leave off the breaking and entering and stick with what we're good at."

"There's not much fun in picking pockets."

"There's not much fun in falling down a chimney or being brained by a hammer."

Frayne sighed, "Alright, Adam, no more breaking and entering. For now."

"For now." Adam knew that it was the best he would get.

CHAPTER SIX

Adam was laughing. Earlier in the day, Frayne had stolen a purse, not a hefty purse by any means, but one that contained the most coins that Adam had seen in months. "To the taverns where 'we shall drink down all unkindness'!" He laughed, staggering as though he were already drunk. They hurried towards the nearest pub, but to his surprise, Frayne stopped before they reached the door.

Adam turned, a quizzical smile tugging at his lips, "Coming Mate?".

Frayne gently rubbed his palms together and took two small steps backwards, "Nah, I don't fancy a drink." His voice was one of studied nonchalance.

Adam laughed incredulously, "What kind of man doesn't fancy a drink?" But he stopped at the fierce look in Frayne's eyes. Memory had darkened them as an image, buried long ago, crept to the forefront of his mind.

Once again, he was waiting on slick cobblestones, staring up at the tavern that Trudy had entered hours before. She lurched out the door, seemingly oblivious to

Frayne's presence mere metres in front of her.

"Mum," he stepped forward, tentatively reaching for her arm, "I've come…come to take you home."

She saw him then—her beady eyes narrowed to slits as she squinted through the drink-induced fog towards her son. "Don't you never," her hand and her voice rose with alarming speed, "never," she swayed, and the hand missed its small target, "call me that. You are not my son."

Those final five words, hissed rather than shouted, pierced into Frayne's heart and hurt him more than her hand ever could.

He blinked back the darkness. Adam now stood before him, fear and uncertainty mingling upon his face.

"It's fine." Frayne put on an affected smile, "Drink don't agree with me, is all. I'll wait here." He held up the smile, but the shadow still lingered on his face as he watched Adam disappear through the doors.

It was dark when Adam finally emerged, still laughing and more than slightly drunk. Frayne steadied him, a wicked smile flashing across his face, "'Why, sir, for my part I say the gentleman had drunk himself out of his five sentences.'"

Adam grinned, "Know what I like more than the great Shakespeare himself? You. You're a good man, Frayne. Fifteen years on earth, and I've never met anyone better. I think." Here, he endeavoured to pat Frayne on the back but found the act upset his balance and settled for collapsing into a giggling heap upon the cobbles instead. Frayne simply gazed at him in amused bewilderment.

Adam awoke long after the sun swept over the rooftop upon which he slept. He cautiously opened his eyes to see Frayne before him, contemplatively chewing on a hunk of bread.

Frayne looked down at him, "How d'you feel?"

Adam moaned and murmured through hesitant lips, "'O thou invisible spirit of wine, if thou hast no name to be known by, let us call thee devil.'"

"I've had an idea," Frayne stated.

Adam struggled into a sitting position and directed his attention towards Frayne with as much enthusiasm as he could muster.

"I've been thinking…"

"Dangerous thing that."

"Shut up, lemme finish." Frayne smirked, "We can't live on the streets forever. Pickpocketing is fine day-to-day, but we've got to do something more. We must become gentlemen." Adam gaped at him. "We shall not become authentic gentlemen—we are too far beneath that—but men trust those graced with the appearance of gentlemen. It will give us a badge of credibility, if you will, and shall elevate us to the higher circles where thievery becomes ever more profitable."

Adam groaned, "You're talking like a king again. I thought you were shot of that."

Frayne sighed with irritation, "Look at us, Adam. We look like thieves, like beggars. We could not get within twelve metres of a gentleman without having the watch called. Gentlemen are rich. If we can get close to them, we could make ourselves rich too."

Adam sighed resignedly, "I'm too hungover to disagree. Whatever you think, Mate."

I will admit, Mr Simmons, that I have made Frayne's time on the streets of his city sound somewhat idyllic. My narrative of that time thus far has been all storybook adventure and mischief, with little real danger highlighted. I have wholly failed to capture the sicknesses, the fights, the agonising brushes with death, and the constant terror that stalked Adam and Frayne. What good does it do to dwell on those things? They were present, as you can so readily imagine, but so were the joys and the harmless mishaps, and it is those that I choose to dwell on. To do otherwise would be to make this a much darker narrative than it needs to be. Frayne's childhood, while crucial to this tale, is not the heart of it. It was a painful time for him and others, and forgive me, it is not one that I would choose to resurrect, even in a story.

CHAPTER SEVEN

Mr Simmons, I now offer you an image. It was one of those glorious summer days that rarely favour our country, and the streets, bereft of shadows, were swathed in sunlight. The splendid houses that lined them glittered as sunbeams admired themselves in glass windows and polished doorknobs. The air filled with the music of horses—black, white, and chestnut—dancing down the road, their heads held high, necks arched. Some pulled rattling carriages through the open curtains of which one could glimpse faces adorned in smiles as rare as the sunshine that inspired them. Figures dotted the pavements, their brightly coloured silks and chintzes suggesting to one on a level with the birds that they were nothing more than carefully placed jewels.

Through this idyllic scene, two gentlemen strolled. The taller of the two was cloaked in a fine silk suit, the colour of which was a perfect match for his ebony hair and eyes. The darkness of his attire set him apart from the brightly coloured figures about him. He carried himself with calm dignity, but the vaguely amused glint in his eye and the slight smile that played on his lips suggested that, as he walked, he was enjoying some great and private jest.

His companion's suit lacked the severity of the former and was, in a bizarrely erratic manner, more in keeping with those around him. The suit was an eclectic mix of vibrant colours, but despite its garish design, the wearer somehow made it appear dapper. His step was lively with a barely contained verve, and beneath his charming expression lay a wild restlessness as though—were it not for the constraints of his suit—he would break apart and fly away into whirlwinds of life.

Such perfect scenes rarely last longer than the brief moment it takes to appreciate them, and this was no exception. The calm was broken by a woman flinging wide one of the freshly painted doors, an expression of panicked excitement sketched upon her face. She rushed down the few steps that led to the path but tripped over skirts which were not made for such haste and tumbled onto the two passing gentlemen.

Adam stumbled, cursing, as the woman fairly knocked him off his feet, then almost succeeded in pulling Frayne over with him as he reached out to steady himself. Frayne, who had stepped away just in time to avoid the worst of the collision, now rushed forward to aid the unfortunate woman. She had landed in an undignified heap of limbs and skirts, scandalised glances, and nervous titters. She pushed Frayne's hands away roughly, then with curses almost as eloquent as Adam's, gathered her voluminous skirts and rose to her feet. She paused to brush at some imagined speck of dirt before raising her golden head to convey the full weight of her furious embarrassment to the two gentlemen. She froze, mouth opened as though to deliver a scolding, but the words lay forgotten upon her tongue, and her hostile expression melted away into surprise. "Frayne?" Farrah asked.

Now, as unlikely as this reunion may seem, Mr Simmons, in all honesty, it is, of course, not wholly impossible. Frayne had long abandoned any expectation of seeing Farrah again, but the same was not true for her. As Frayne had expected, the workhouse had torn hard at Farrah's spirit. Her naivety—born and nurtured during her sheltered life with her mother—was quickly devastated, and she was left empty and aghast at the discovery that the world she lived in was cold, bitter, and callous. A life of drudgery and destitution is not fit for any child but may prove especially detrimental to one with a heart as freshly broken as her own. The suffering bestowed upon her had the potential to steal her vitality away and render her, like so many others, a broken, hollowed-out child with empty eyes and a shattered spirit.

There were three things, I believe, that kept Farrah whole: the first was the unwavering fire of her character that raged against the despair that threatened to engulf her spirit. The second was the teachings of her mother that stood as a barrier between the world's cruelty and her soul. Finally, Farrah found hope in the knowledge that somewhere beyond the bleak walls of her confinement was a bright-spirited boy who believed in his heart that she was a Lady and loved her still.

Mr Simmons, is it so odd that when Farrah came of age and left the workhouse, she moved to the city where she believed her dearest friend on earth lived? And wishing him to have escaped a fate such as her own and found wealth and happiness, is it not natural that she should seek employment in the most affluent area of the city? And if she spent her precious few free hours wandering the streets, her lonely heart cupped in her hands, searching each passing face for the dark features she remembered so well, who are we to judge her? It is our dreams, improbable though they may seem, that give us motivation and hope. We hold them like a candle in the darkness until we see them fulfilled or until the wick burns out.

Perhaps fate had a hand in their meeting again—upon reflection, it certainly seems that the chaotic, arduous, and often circumstantial web of Frayne's life would have brought the Fates great delight. Whatever the case, on that bright summer day, eight years after their mother's death, their paths crossed again.

CHAPTER EIGHT

Adam scowled down into his ale. Farrah had led them to the taproom of an inn—the sort of inn with clean floors and respectable customers that still made Adam feel ill at ease. Frayne had explained his past connection with her in a jumbled and distracted manner which increased Adam's sense of agitation. He could feel resentment and apprehension fermenting with the ale in his stomach, rising into a wave of churlish anger that clouded his thoughts.

"So, you're the one who made him talk like a bleeding king?"

Farrah, who had been deep in conversation with Frayne, paused mid-sentence. "Beg pardon?"

"Adam," Frayne began but was interrupted by his friend's loud sigh, quickly followed by a stifled belch.

"I know, I know." Adam muttered, then rolling his eyes, turned to Farrah, "I humbly beg your forgiveness, 'rude am I in my speech, and little blessed with the soft phrase of peace'."

She squinted slightly towards him, unsure if he was mocking her.

"I merely intended," Adam continued in a slower tone, "to enquire whether you were responsible for dear Frayne's education when he was a boy? I knew him before you see, and was rather taken aback by his...favourable change in mannerisms."

Though she was perplexed by Adam's speech, Farrah could feel an unexpected excitement rising within her. She and Frayne had never spoken about his early life, and though now she was old enough to guess much of it, an old curiosity still tugged at her heart. Had this peculiarly dressed gentleman truly known Frayne before he had come into her life?

Several questions fought to reach her lips first, but Farrah pushed them back. Adam's hostile tone was now unmistakable, and she was not one to allow a gentleman to get the better of her. She raised her head to better view Adam at the end of her nose, "I believe…Sir, that change came at the hands of my mother. Moreover, you are clearly drunk and should keep your ill-mannered words to yourself. I am a lady and will not be addressed in such a boorish manner." With a pointed glare, she turned away from him and redirected her attention back towards Frayne.

Adam could think of no reasonable response to this, so he settled for sputtering indignantly for a moment before hoisting himself from his seat and stalking over to the bar—his colourful suit and stiff manner making him look like an affronted peacock. It took all of Frayne's considerable willpower not to laugh aloud. Until this point, he had kept his eyes firmly trained upon Farrah, but the sight of Adam cuffing patrons with his voluminous sleeves as he gestured for his drink was hard to ignore.

The distraction did not last long, and Frayne returned his attention to Farrah with a gentle smile, "You have changed, Farrah."

She laughed, but there was some sadness in her eyes, "I should think so. It has been many years since we have seen each other, and I could not stay a little girl forever. Nor you, a little boy. You have grown much Frayne."

"Yes, Adam is fond of telling me so. I think he may resent my height." He glanced over at the ever-so-slightly shorter man who stood hunched over the bar, "But you have grown even more beautiful. Your face is so much like your mother's now."

Farrah smiled and blushed, but Frayne saw she was ill at ease. She looked away to speak with a passing barmaid, and Frayne studied her face more intently, curious to see what changes time had wrought in his friend.

Farrah had grown, of course, but still retained her lively step, which seemed incongruous with the dignified, almost haughty manner in which she carried herself. Her hair, still long and golden, was swept elegantly back from her face to frame her dusty green eyes. A slight hardness around the corners of her mouth had developed, and the suspicious looks she cast about her were certainly new, but her smile, when it showed, was unchanged, and the light in her face undimmed.

Frayne longed to ask her about her life. Farrah's broken words of goodbye, spoken as he left their home years before, still rang in his ears, and he wished to know everything that had happened to her since that moment. But he knew without asking that many of the days that had passed since then had been painful for her, and the burdens she now carried were not easy ones to speak of.

The scars adversity leaves upon a person are most obvious to those who have endured similar hardships. Though Farrah did not try to hide the signs of her past pain, Frayne noticed them as only a fellow sufferer would.

They were evident in her hurried movements, in the way she almost imperceptibly shied away from the strangers around her, in the tight fold of her arms against her front, and in her eyes that, beneath the thin covering of delight, seemed somehow fractured. She wore her brokenness with quiet pride, knowing that it was an indication of all she had overcome and the strength that had carried her there. Looking into her face, so like her mother's, Frayne was filled with bitter admiration.

Farrah returned her attention to him and likewise studied his face with a sense of mingled joy and remorse. When she spoke, only the barest hint of regret coloured her voice. "I am pleased you have done well for yourself Frayne." She smiled, "You look like a true gentleman now. But how did you secure such a patron as this gentleman here?" She turned to Adam, now returned to the table and in considerably better spirits since he had exchanged his empty cup for a full one.

Even without a drink, Adam could not maintain his displeasure for any long period, and he broke out into uproarious laughter. "'Since every jack became a gentleman, there's many a gentle person made a jack.' Take heed, Frayne, and remember the good lady's words when next you see fit to censure my grammar. A gentleman, she calls me! And your patron! Although I believe," here turning back to Farrah, "you are not entirely mistaken in naming me Frayne's patron. I have supported him for much of my life, and I ought to take credit for much of his current state—his ability to breathe, for instance, is all thanks to me. For if it were not for my most timely and generous aid, not to mention my outstanding prowess in defending the weak, the dear boy here would be lying dead in a gutter."

"And you, my friend," Frayne smiled at the grinning Adam, "would still be lying senseless on a barroom floor."

"Irrelevant, dear Sir, irrelevant!" Adam exclaimed at this point, seemingly oblivious to Farrah's presence.

"It seems," she broke in smiling, "that Frayne has a penchant for gutters. But pray tell, if not for a patron, how did you come to possess your current wealth? Surely your suit alone is worth a gentleman's fortune."

Adam threw a smug glance at Frayne, "I told you. Did I not tell you it would be so? 'For the apparel oft proclaims the man,' and in this instance, the apparel proclaims the man a liar, even if all are blind to it but I."

Frayne gave an almost imperceptible roll of his eyes, "Adam possesses a touch of the dramatic."

"A most generous way of putting it!" Adam interrupted.

"Nevertheless, he is right. My friend is a master of guise and deceit." Frayne continued.

"And proud of it, never doubt it, Sir!"

Farrah followed this exchange with some degree of bewilderment.

Frayne, seeing her confusion, flushed faintly. "Adam was insinuating, and rightly so, that our clothes, in truth, our whole personas, are somewhat poorer than one may first perceive."

Adam nodded sagely, "'The world is still deceived with ornament.'"

Indeed, upon further inspection of their attire, one may have noticed that not all of Frayne's buttons matched, and Adam's brightly coloured necktie concealed a tear in the cloth beneath it. Certainly, their clothing had once been fine and worth a small fortune, I doubt not, but those days were long past, though it did not readily show.

"Ah," Farrah's lips quirked upward at the corners, "you gentlemen are imposters."

"Worse, dear lady." Adam sighed before Frayne could interpose, "We are the basest of men, the most common of criminals. We are nought but petty thieves trying to make our way in this world."

Farrah gave a short bark of laughter, "More than petty thieves if your apparel is any indication."

Frayne shifted uncomfortably, remembering the disapproval that Farrah had once held towards thievery. His embarrassment was quickly forgotten, however, when his gaze fixed on a figure standing by the bar at the far end of the taproom.

Adam followed Frayne's stare and sighed. "Let it go, Mate," he murmured, "'s not worth it." But Frayne didn't hesitate and, in a moment, was halfway across the room, leaving Adam's words dying in his throat.

A man swayed in front of the bar, words slurred but no less forceful and punctuated quite effectively by a small blade that he waved at the stout innkeeper before him.

"Bleeding innkeepers charging me more for board than God does the angels, filling the beer with water so it tastes like…" was all Adam heard before Frayne smartly smacked the knife from the man's hand and rapidly twisted the drunk's arms behind him until he was bent double–spitting and swearing, but neatly incapacitated. In a moment, the man was out of the door, and Frayne was cooly depositing a handful of coins upon the polished bar.

Adam groaned and lowered his head to his hands, "Will that fool ever learn to let things go?! That drunken arse was richer than the both of us, but he paid for his drinks!"

"Where did he learn that?" Farrah was watching Frayne curiously.

"What, paying for arses?"

"No, the,"

"Oh, the arm thing?" Adam waved his hands in exasperation, "Trudy used to do it to him all the time.

Bleeding drunks."

"Who is Trudy?"

Adam paused mid-curse, "Trudy? You mean he never mentioned…"

Frayne returned then, his movements carefully controlled and darkness growing in his eyes. Adam knew that he was remembering cold cobblestones and his mother's fists. Frayne had never told him of those times, but Adam knew. The whole village had known, but Adam had understood better than most.

The prudent course of action in these moments was to divert Frayne's attention, so Adam turned to Farrah, grinning wickedly. "Now then, what does the lady hide?" he exclaimed, seizing a small parcel that was partially concealed amongst her skirts.

Wide-eyed with panic, Farrah vainly tried to snatch it back. Adam laughed, delighted by the game, "It is rather hefty to be handkerchiefs, and what more would an honourable lady feel the burden to carry? Surely not gold, 'Yellow, glittering, precious gold...' such a thing would be far too tawdry for one such as yourself!"

Ignoring her vehement protests and attempts to retrieve it from him, Adam deftly unwrapped the package and, with a flourish, revealed its contents. A collection of small, elegantly engraved, crested silver spoons lay within. Just as quickly, Adam returned them to their wrappings—his expression shocked and his eyes darting to the tables around them.

Farrah was laughing, and to her surprise, Frayne was also. She turned to Adam, her eyes widening into a look of dramatised innocence. She sighed, "Dear Sir, I am the basest of women, the most common of criminals. I am nought but a petty thief trying to make my way in this world."

Adam tossed her a look of grudging respect.

"Where are you gentlemen boarding?" she asked Frayne.

He smiled at her, "Here it seems."

"Then I shall stay here also."

Adam watched as Frayne escorted Farrah to the bar, and he slowly allowed his smile to drop. Cold tendrils were wrapping themselves tightly around his heart. She would be trouble, he knew it. She was a faery charming a demon, and she would win him in the end. She would steal Frayne away and Adam would be left, cold, broken, and painfully alone.

CHAPTER NINE

It was early when Farrah left the inn the next morning. A light rain spattered the streets, and she stepped from the warm taproom with hesitation, a thick cloak held closely about her shoulders. She did not notice Adam's slim, pale face regarding her from an upstairs window. Moments later, Adam and Frayne slipped out of the inn behind her and began following her progress, winding between the few passersby that traversed the streets at that early hour, the sleep not yet washed from their faces by the morning sun.

The three figures quickly left the clean comforts of the inn behind them as they moved towards a darker and more squalid section of the city. It had taken much effort for Frayne to persuade Adam that the best method of stalking Farrah was by remaining on ground level at a discreet distance, and not by scrambling after her on the low, slippery rooftops that lined the streets. It was not that Adam was reckless or impractical by any means, but occasionally, he forgot that he was no longer an urchin at home in the city.

We are quick to romanticise the past, and though Adam's life of poverty had once seemed to him a tragedy akin to those penned by his idol, there were moments still when he longed to return to it. Most days, he desired nothing more than to cast off the constraints of his finery and run once again over the rooftops of his city. He missed the freedom, the exhilaration, and the feeling that he was the only person in the world. I imagine Adam had been his most fae-like in those moments, perched high above the rest of the world. It is not difficult to picture him, running barefoot across the slate, never faltering despite his precarious position, wild straw hair flying from his face, pale eyes wide, teeth bared in a grin, and a laugh too wild to describe, tearing from his lips. But I digress.

Farrah soon reached her destination, a small, out-of-the-way shop—the kind of place that one might pass by a dozen times but never deign to glance in at the window. Frayne and Adam paused to watch her duck inside, unsure if they should follow.

Frayne shook his head, "It is only a shop, Adam, let's go back." But if Adam heard, he paid no heed and quickly followed Farrah. Frayne hesitated, but only for a moment before he hurried after Adam.

As he ran across the road towards the door of the shop, concern for Farrah mingled with Frayne's curiosity. Finding her again felt like he was reuniting with an old friend and meeting someone new. Gone was the bright child that Frayne had known. In her place stood a stranger, with mere tendrils of her old self weaving through her like threads of sunshine. The small, enthusiastic girl enshrined in his heart and mind remained there still but seemed quite at odds with this new figure. He knew very little about Farrah now and nothing about her life since he had seen her last. Nevertheless, he hoped that in time, if there would be time, he would find her to be less changed than he imagined.

As Adam marched up the street towards the small shop, he felt no concern, merely curiosity. His feelings of anxious hostility from the night before had not fully abated. Although deep within his heart, he knew that no good could come from following Farrah, he was determined to continue anyway. There was little justification or explanation on his part for following her, at least none that he would admit to Frayne, but perhaps there was still a chance it would all turn out for the best. Adam grinned, perhaps they would discover Farrah in a covert meeting with a secret lover, and all his fears from the night before would be allayed.

He burst into the shop with an unnecessary flourish to find Farrah in close conversation with a slight woman behind a bench. A scowl rapidly replaced Farrah's expression of surprise, but Adam, seemingly unperturbed, maintained his grin and happily exclaimed, "Madam, this was entirely Frayne's idea."

Frayne elbowed past his companion, "Farrah…" he faltered at the fierceness in her eyes, then pressed onward, "We were concerned, we thought that perhaps you may be in trouble, we…" his voice subsided. What had happened to his eloquent words, his easy speeches?

"I do not require your concern, I do not require your help, and I do not need your interference in my life."

Something about the low, measured pace of her voice cut him, and he remembered—a memory he had suppressed for so long—the dark attic, the low whisper, the familiar pain in his heart, "I hate you, Frayne."

He tightened his jaw and turned away from her, "I am sorry to have troubled you, Madam. Let us leave, Adam. We are not wanted here."

A light touch on his arm stopped him. Pain and regret washed over Farrah's face. "Frayne, I am sorry, I am so accustomed to…" She paused and shook her head, "I did not mean it. I appreciate your willingness to help. Please, come and meet Dahlia."

Frayne nodded and smiled slightly, though his heart still felt cold. Dahlia had remained silent throughout this exchange, though her eyes had moved nervously from one speaker to the other, and she had edged out from behind the bench and closer to Farrah.

Dahlia was small, with dark hair that stood in stark contrast to the vivid blue of her eyes and the paleness of her skin. She was lovely, and Adam felt as though Shakespeare would have given his life to compose a sonnet for her. Then again, Adam felt the same way about every lovely woman he met, and it was with a smirk that Frayne watched him bow deeply towards Dahlia.

Frayne had spent many hours attempting to teach Adam the art of bowing, a skill that any accomplished gentleman must master. Adam delighted in the concept yet unceasingly failed in the execution. His motions were exaggerated, his balance shaky, and the overall effect rendered him less than debonaire. Regardless, when Adam flashed Dahlia a charming (if slightly devilish) grin mid-bow, Frayne knew that the comical aspect of the gesture was lost on her.

"Dahlia and I work as a partnership." Farrah continued, "She helps me sell the items I acquire."

"Her?" Adam's eyes widened with gleeful surprise, "She is your fence? But she is a woman!" Adam never did have the capacity to retain a woman's interest.

"A woman makes a better and more trustworthy partner in these endeavours." Farrah's tone had dropped again, "One may trust a woman not to knock one down for the sake of a spoon. A woman will not cheat or report one to the authorities. I would trust Dahlia with my life."

Adam's face was red with contrition, but Frayne could tell that the idea still amused him. He was sure that the prospect of a lovely woman involved in such clandestine acts brought great delight to Adam.

If you will excuse me, Mr Simmons, I would like to address a few matters concerning Farrah. From this encounter, it may seem that she had become a somewhat harsh, quick-tempered woman. I ask that you forgive her for her outbursts and not consider her such, as any severity in her manner was born from suffering and shame. Her cruel life had taught her to respond first with anger and coldness, and her reaction was instinctive rather than deliberate.

In truth, Farrah was ashamed of what her life had become and afraid of how Frayne might judge her. She longed to be the person she was when he had first known her—joyful, lighthearted, and innocently strong. It was a light that still burned within her, but she had covered it, for to shine such a light in the world in which she existed was to invite trouble. It was a light so long shrouded, that its existence was eventually forgotten, even by herself.

CHAPTER TEN

I wish to move ahead some weeks as the interim, while pleasant, is of little concern to the progress of this narrative. Farrah's introduction of Dahlia had opened several possibilities to Frayne. A reliable fence was a rare asset, and although his ventures with Adam were profitable, the addition of Farrah would expand their opportunities immensely.

It soon became apparent that for many years, Farrah had been supporting herself by stealing the odd treasure from the homes or pockets of gentlemen. "Every one of them deserved it." she assured Frayne, "Offensive, scheming, grasping men. Each would rather condemn every man on earth to poverty than relinquish a single coin."

It had never particularly occurred to Frayne to consider the manner of man, or woman, for that matter, that he stole from. To him, thievery was a game and provided he trusted those he played it with, he did not pause to wonder about those he played against. Farrah was not so impersonal. As Adam had expected, Frayne was becoming increasingly charmed by her, and he vowed to himself that, from now on, they would only steal from those whom Farrah deemed deserving.

One cannot imagine the amount of devising and strategizing that went into their first operation together. Frayne insisted that they consider every possible outcome meticulously, and Farrah demanded that Dahlia be present for every meeting to offer advice and pose questions. After a time, these meetings became rather merry affairs—with food and laughter present in equal measures. Farrah and Dahlia talked and bantered together as only dear friends could while Adam flung outrageous compliments at Dahlia and teased Farrah. Frayne laughed as he had not laughed for years, matching Adam's jests and heaping ridiculous flattery upon both women. He became animated in a way that only showed when some grand plan was racing through his mind, lending dynamism to his body.

By the end of the month, they had devised a rather clever plot, which circumstances favoured more than Frayne could have ever imagined. Farrah knew of the impending wedding of a gentleman whose full name and title must, for now, escape me. In this narrative, I shall refer to him as Edward. Edward's new wife was a woman of most prodigious means, and Farrah, having heard rumours of her infamous temperament, assured Frayne that the couple would make the ideal target. "She is a frivolous, bad-tempered thing, and whatever she wishes for, she receives."

Upon first visiting her beloved's townhouse, the lady was most displeased to note the lack of competent staff and commented, "What may suit a bachelor of adequate means certainly will not suit a married gentleman. Why, Edward, how shall I host even the smallest dinner parties? Am I expected to slave in the kitchen as a scullery maid?"

So, Edward, quite to his wife's most vocal relief, spoke

to his steward, who, together with the housekeeper, went about the arduous task of hiring additional and reliable help. So, the plot began with Farrah, her hair pulled tightly behind her head, a plain, ugly coloured frock hanging at odd angles about her person, references clutched in her hand (most fabricated, but some authentic), and a slightly vacant, docile smile adorning her face.

As always, Adam was the first to laugh, "'See where she comes, appareled like the spring'!"

Farrah threw a scarf at him, "Mock all you wish, for I will be wealthy by the end of this."

Adam examined the scarf, "A favour! The scullery maid graces me with a favour!"

Even Frayne had difficulty hiding his smile.

During that first month of marriage, Edward's quiet townhouse was thrown into an uproar as every floorboard was scrubbed, every bit of wallpaper and carpet torn away and replaced, and many expensive, frivolous things brought in to replace the old books and worn leather armchairs that had previously leant a sort of comfortable charm to the place. Now that the house was in a state of fashion acceptable to Mrs Edward, the second month was given over to costumes and cuisine. Tailors flew in and out of the house, and boxes and packages were delivered with an alarming rapidity. Down in the kitchens, an increasingly bad-tempered cook was besieged by a flood of new recipes, each more extravagant than the last. Above it all, echoed the shrill voice of the house's mistress drowned only by her husband's voice calling for his manservant to hurry with his drink.

During that second month, Adam entered the scene in the guise of a tailor. He burst into the townhouse in a flurry with a crowd of other tailors and seamstresses—his hair swept into disarray, his movements hasty and erratic. He moved about the room in a whirl, measuring Mrs Edward's limbs, throwing scraps of cloth at anyone who got in his way, calling out measurements and colours, and shouting at the other tailors and their bemused attendants. He left with his arms full of silks, velvets, and laces that he certainly hadn't entered with and promises for the finest dresses Mrs Edwards had ever seen. The lady was immensely satisfied.

In the third month, the house came into its own, as party after party was held. Relatives, friends, dignitaries, and the occasional well-dressed stranger were ushered in, fed, entertained, admired, and waved out without a single meaningful word exchanged. Frayne and Dahlia were amongst the elegant crowd. Both were dressed in fine style and carried themselves with such condescending dignity that by the end of the evening, there was not a single guest present who would have admitted they were not acquainted with them by one means or another. They danced, smiled, gossiped, and left with pockets full of crystal, jewellery, and the occasional silken handkerchief. It was a month of brightly coloured dresses, fabulous dishes, and disingenuous laughter, and throughout it all, Edward's wife felt as though her life had been nothing before this glorious season. What Edward thought of these events was a mystery to all but his tumbler of whiskey.

The beginning of the fourth month marked the end of Mrs Edward's glorious season and the coup de grâce of Frayne's plan. It was put into motion by Farrah, the kitchen maid. After spending the better part of the day running errands for the afflicted cook, she returned to find the kitchen long emptied of staff. As planned, she set the stove aflame, then doused it with oil to encourage the burning. Moments later, Frayne and Adam, waiting on the street, let out a great cry of "Help, fire!" before hastily entering the house.

If all had gone according to plan, the fire would have been doused before it left the kitchen, but Farrah was unaware that the cook secreted a few bottles of spirits in a small cupboard next to the oven. With a great rush of flame, the fire grew until it leapt from the kitchen and spread to the rest of the rooms on the lower floor. Adam escorted a shrieking Mrs Edward outside, closely followed by her stunned husband and retinue of servants, before hurrying back inside to face the conflagration.

Frayne immediately went in search of Farrah. He found her with several neighbours, desperately trying to extinguish the flames.

"Are you hurt?" he asked, pulling her aside, concern etched across his face.

She shook her head and smiled at the streaks of soot adorning his nose, "Not hurt, but here, help me to wrap my hands up. It will seem strange if I come out unscathed after spending so much time indoors, and the bandages will hide these little silver spoons very nicely."

Frayne grinned at the sight of the six small, crested spoons she held clutched in her hands.

As one may expect, the worst damage occurred in the kitchen and adjoining rooms, however, once the danger passed, Adam began the process of removing "charred and damaged" items from the rooms upstairs so that the mistress of the house would not be "unduly distressed by the destruction". Finally, the spectacle was over, and after being tended to with cooling cloths and a great deal of brandy, Mrs Edward threw aside her aides and called for her carriage with only a slight hysteria tingeing her voice. She flung herself inside, ordered her husband to follow her, "immediately after this mess has been dealt with", and clattered away, never to return.

On the whole, the four conspirators enjoyed themselves immensely. The material rewards alone were cause enough for celebration, but the sense of exhilaration they experienced as they concluded their venture was unmatched. That evening, they gathered together in a room of the inn. Adam adorned himself with articles of stolen clothing and danced around the room, singing a song of his own conception in a warbling falsetto and flinging scraps of vibrant silks at Dahlia. She soon accompanied him, and they whirled, leapt, and stumbled while Frayne beat out an enthusiastic rhythm with his feet that was completely at odds with Adam's tune.

For a moment, Farrah understood Frayne's passion for larceny. It was a desire for adventure, to stand before danger and then evade it, but more importantly for Frayne, thievery created the opportunity to escape from his sorrow and the poverty that had plagued him for so long. It gave him a sense of hope for his future, a hope that ushered in joy to light his darkness. Farrah knew that it was a light that he would pursue until the day he died.

As she watched jubilation paint itself in bright colours over Frayne's face, Farrah knew that she had linked her fate with his. She would scheme and steal for as long as he did, and she would find joy in it because they would be together. The little wraith her mother had brought into their home so long ago had grown into this brilliant, shining man, and Farrah had given him her heart. He was the only person left in the world who brought light into her darkness, and she knew it was a light that she would pursue until the day she died.

Dahlia and Adam were still spinning around the small room. Dizzy and laughing, they eventually collapsed onto the wooden floor. Dahlia smiled to see Farrah deep in conversation with Frayne. They looked well together, and she was happy for her friend. She glanced back at Adam. He had pulled himself into a sitting position and gazed at her face.

"'I do love nothing in the world as well as you—is not that strange?'" He murmured.

Dahlia was surprised by his intensity but quickly composed her features and cast him a dubious look, "Shakespeare may have pretty words, but I would rather hear Adam's."

"'Let me be that I am and seek not to alter me', Dahlia. I use Shakespeare's words to voice that which is in my heart that my own words do not satisfy. Do not doubt that just because one man spoke them before me they are any less my own."

"But you quote lovers and villains as though you pay no heed to the manner of man for whom those words were created."

"As far as I am concerned, Dahlia, those words were created for none but me." He watched her for a while longer. "Do you not trust me?"

Her composed expression faltered, and for a moment, Adam saw that deep within her remained a portion of the small, anxious child she had once been.

He smiled gently at her, "You must have confidence, Dahlia and carry it with you like a stone in your heart."

"A stone?" She trailed off, confused.

"Like a pebble that you collect from the beach to carry in your palm. Smooth, solid, and comfortable. Tested by the sea and warmed by the sun, keep it with you always, and it will ground you." He grinned at her then with an expression full of hope, love, and wild abandon.

She shook her head but could not help smiling back at

him. And who could fault her? For all his impish peculiarities, Adam was charming.

CHAPTER ELEVEN

Three months later, they began again. Not long after the conclusion of their first theft, Farrah suggested that they repeat the same formula on a different target. Though Frayne and Adam were initially hesitant to try the same trick twice, it did not take much effort to change their minds. They all craved the thrill they had experienced when robbing Edward and his wife, and as Frayne expressed, "Last time was merely a test, imagine how much more we can improve, how many other ploys we can devise within this same method."

So, Farrah donned the garb of a kitchen girl again and left to apply for work. This time, their target was a young man of great inheritance. He had been raised lacking nothing. As a child, if he wished for a treat, decadent cakes sculpted into pretty shapes were brought to him. As a young man, if he desired a horse, his father would spend a small fortune on the finest creature money could buy. The extravagance was sickening, and the boy suffered for it. He grew up to be a man of weak character and great pride, scorning the world and all those in it.

All patience, even that of a parent, comes to an end, and the young man's father had sent him to the city to "gain some experience of life". The young man himself had no qualms about the arrangement. He intended to spend a few happy months enjoying the city's vices, before returning to the comforts and luxuries of home.

"I think that I may despise him more than both Edward and his wife combined." Farrah expressed one day. "Such a cruel, pompous, egotistical fop the world has never seen. Did you realise that within the short time he has been here, he has already impregnated two of his maids? I shall carry a knife, and what pleasure I shall take in using it should the need arise."

Adam almost choked with laughter.

Fortunately for the young man, the need did not arise, as he never deigned to venture into the lower levels of his house. Everything went smoothly. Adam reprised his role as a flustered, erratic tailor. He found great delight in throwing pieces of silk suits in the gentleman's face and occasionally pricking the unfortunate fop with little silver pins. Frayne and Dahlia attended most, if not all, the parties that the gentleman threw. Their host was far too inebriated at each event to notice if strangers slipped in or if his guests slipped out with various belongings of his cloaked in their garments or tucked discreetly into a purse.

Overall, it seemed that this venture would prove to be even more profitable than their first. Their victim's extravagance and general state of mental oblivion and carelessness made him the ideal target. They carried on their ploy for a month longer than they had with Edward and seemed only to prosper from it. It wasn't until the fifth month when they knew that the young gentleman was preparing to return home, that Farrah went about the task of setting his house on fire. All went without incident, and though this fire was more controlled than the first, more damage was inflicted upon the house than had been done to Edwards'. More belongings were damaged, more carpets singed, and the large portrait of the house's owner that had graced the foyer for months was reduced to a heap of ashes and a few charred scraps of canvas.

The young gentleman stood on the street watching as flames engulfed his house. He reeled away from the men—common men—who were rushing with buckets of water to save his property. He turned, stunned and outraged at the unfairness of it all, and stumbled, knocking over a small kitchen maid who had just come out of the building. Cheeks tear-stained, hands bandaged, she fell to the cobblestones, and four small silver spoons tumbled from her skirts. Rough hands seized Farrah. She screamed once for Frayne, but he was gone.

The cell was cold. Cold, dank, horrible. Cliches rushed through Farrah's mind as she sat on the stone floor. There was a bed, but she preferred the floor. In truth, the cell was not as appalling as she had imagined it would be. It was dry, and though chilly, the sun streamed through the narrow-barred window and staved off true cold. Although the bed most likely housed one or two lice, the sheets were neither stained nor threadbare, but despite these luxuries, Farrah felt that she had sunk to depths she had never been to before.

A thin line of red adorned her cheek. When the gentleman noticed the fallen spoons, he pulled her up by her hair, and she spat at him. He had hit her then. It was a long time since she was last struck, and the cruel slap brought with it a rush of shame and despair that she hadn't felt since she was a girl in the workhouse. His ring had cut her, and now she thoughtfully smeared the line of blood with her fingers, painting a swirling pattern of pain onto the canvas of her face. She stopped and rubbed it away. Vague concerns for Frayne and Adam danced at the back of her mind, but nothing other than apathy accompanied her musings as to her own fate.

Four silver spoons. That was all that they had found, but it was enough. She felt like a Judas. Thirty pieces of silver? For her, four was enough. She had betrayed her mother and the young girl she had once been, the young girl who had turned down a life with the boy she loved because she would not steal. The boy she loved, was that the first time she had admitted that truth to herself? Farrah sighed and closed her eyes. What did it matter? Despair and guilt had welled up within her, and she felt hollow inside. She was alone, and though the cell was lonely, she was grateful there was no one to see her cry.

Farrah opened her eyes. There wasn't much difference, open or closed, as it was dark now. Her muscles ached, and one of her arms was numb. Had she slept? She had not intended to. Her limbs spasmed in protest when she moved, so she remained still, though the floor was uncomfortable. A faint scratching sound emanated from beyond her window. Was that what had awoken her? She told herself not to care, but a small flame of hope rose within her, and she struggled to sit. The sound stopped—it must have been a bird. But then again, this time accompanied by a whisper of her name.

"Frayne?" her voice was as quiet as his.

"Farrah? Thank God." More scuffling, a loud, prolonged scraping, then through the bars of the window came Frayne.

It had taken quite a feat of effort on Frayne's part to reach that point. He had seen the nobleman strike Farrah, and at that moment, it had required all of Adam's power to convince him that attacking her captors outright was a poor idea. Instead, they retreated to the inn, where they and Dahlia cobbled together a rescue plan. Adam, with his usual flair, was all in favour of breaking down doors or tunnelling through the prison ceiling to reach Farrah's cell. Dahlia offered the somewhat more pragmatic approach of using a ladder to access the window of the prison's temporary holding cell on the second floor, where they assumed Farrah was being held. Eventually, they agreed that both methods would be unnecessarily conspicuous, so after dark, Frayne implemented his own plan.

The outside wall of the prison was constructed from large, rectangular stones, with just enough of a gap between each to allow an experienced climber to scale it with some difficulty. Upon reaching the window, Frayne anchored himself there with a rope while he used a small saw to remove one of the wooden bars, allowing himself just enough space to enter the room. It was simple, painful, and perhaps, Mr Simmons, you may imagine he accomplished it too easily. However, before Frayne, few prison escapes had been successfully managed. Measures were certainly in place to prevent prisoners from breaking out, but not so much from breaking in. Frayne was helped in that Farrah was placed—not in a secure cell for the long-term keeping of prisoners—but in what could be considered a temporary holding room. Nevertheless, I admit, with some pride, that Frayne inspired many of the additional security efforts that most prisons undertake today.

Frayne made his way cautiously through the room to where Farrah still sat. He reached out tentatively, "Farrah, are you injured?"

The quiet hesitancy in her voice when she answered in the negative did nothing to allay the concern in his.

"Farrah, I saw what happened." Guilt sprang up within him. "I saw that man hit you. I should have been there to stop it. I should have done more…" He trailed off. This would do nothing to help them. "I am sorry I was not there, but we must leave now before anyone comes." He brushed her hair gently back from her face, but she did not move. "Farrah?"

"What would Mother think of us if she could see us now?"

The hollow pain that accompanied the question seemed to steal over Frayne mixing with the guilt he already felt. He sat down heavily beside her, uncertainty in his voice. "I expect that she would understand."

"No, she knew poverty. She understood the desperation that comes from having no hope of feeding oneself. It was desperation that must have only been increased by the responsibility she had to me. But she never once stole, or cheated, or deceived. She never deviated from what she knew in her heart to be right and good. She had the strength and the virtue of an angel. She used to tell me that this world, though fallen from grace, could be made a better one if we do what is right and take care of those in it."

Frayne smiled faintly, "I knew she was an angel from the moment I first saw her. But she understood what I was when she took me in. She knew…my childhood, my mother, my true mother…she may not have known the specifics, but she guessed well. She saw what was inside of me, but she still loved me." The anguish that he had buried within himself so long ago was stirring, the hardness that he had placed over it cracking.

"What is inside of you Frayne?" A dull curiosity filled

her voice.

"Darkness, anger, hatred. I know that Adam sees it within me, though he does not speak of it, and Mother saw it too. But she believed that there was light within all people, and if she saw the darkness in me, then she also saw the light, though I must confess that I struggle to see it. I know, Farrah, that if she is looking upon us now, there is no disappointment or judgement within her, just the hope and love that eternally graced her life. And not the hope that we will become better citizens, but the hope that the light within us will triumph over the darkness and that throughout our lives, we will pursue hope and love, and in that pursuit, find joy."

Farrah smiled slightly, "I have never appreciated how eloquent you are."

He smiled too, "'Words sweetly placed and modestly directed'? Spending years with Adam has its benefits." his smile faded, "I am not a good man, Farrah."

"And I am not a good woman Frayne. Our hearts are too scarred for goodness. But Mother knew that we would need each other. I believe from the first moment she saw you upon her doorstep, she knew. Perhaps together, we may find some semblance of goodness to please the world, some depth of happiness to please ourselves, and some reflection of light to bring joy to our mother."

Frayne smiled and slowly stood, "It seems we have both become poets."

She took his offered hand, and squeezed it, "Adam will weep with joy."

Frayne tied the rope around Farrah and carefully lowered her to the ground. Then, looping the rope back around a bar and tying the two free ends together, he anchored himself long enough to wedge the wooden bar back into place, before slowly climbing to the ground.

Once there, he untied the knot and pulled the rope free from around the bar.

He grinned at Farrah, "For all they will know, you simply vanished from your cell."

She shook her head in amusement, "Either vanished or stolen away by a demon."

He nodded sagely, "I would place my money on the demon.

CHAPTER TWELVE

Adam and Dahlia were waiting for them in the taproom of the inn. The tension in Adam's face eased but did not vanish when he saw Frayne and Farrah enter together. He briefly embraced Farrah, then leaned over to Frayne, "Someone's been waiting for you, Mate." He jerked his head over to the bar. A man stood there, quietly conversing with the innkeeper, his sheepish expression completely at odds with the aggressive face that wore it. Frayne stared at him uncomprehendingly. The man turned as though he could sense the eyes upon him, and his face coloured when he met Frayne's gaze. Adam swore. "He's coming over."

Dahlia and Farrah seemed to share Adam's discomfort, and understandably so. The man was of moderate height and stout, but his stoutness was the sturdy, hulking sort born of hard labour, not overindulgence. Although his figure was threatening, it was the indomitable air with which he carried himself that was truly intimidating. I know of no better way to explain him. He could have been short and willowy, and men would still have shied away from his passing. It was as though the spirit of a giant lived within him, so unassumingly secure in the power that was once his, that his current mortal constraints were of no concern to him. His features were boldly etched and framed in lines, which time had so carefully engraved onto his face to lend it an added ferocity. The muddied brown of his hair and beard were untouched by streaks of silver, and within the darkness of his eyes lay a pain and anger almost animalistic in its intensity. Then, belying it all, was the expression of timidity that still shrouded his face when he reached Frayne.

"You won't remember me," his voice was rich, low, with only a hint of hardness to it, "you er, you threw me out of 'ere. I was drunk, 'ad a knife, shouting at the innkeeper about God knows what, and you stopped me." he gestured to the man behind the bar, "'E said you paid for me."

Frayne nodded in recognition.

"I wouldn't 'ave 'urt 'im, Thomas is a good man, knows me well, knows I get angry, but you did a good thing. I owe you a debt." His speech over, he glanced at the ground, seemingly unsure of what reaction his words would inspire.

Frayne nodded again, "Thank you, I am glad to hear it, I am Frayne".

"Devin." The man grasped Frayne's proffered hand.

"Adam." Adam extended his arm also.

Devin did not smile, but the uncertainty had lifted from his face. Then he turned to Farrah and Dahlia as though noticing them for the first time and hesitated.

"Do you have a family, Devin?" Frayne watched his face closely.

"No," the man's eyes never left the two women, "I 'ad a wife once, a little girl too." He met Frayne's stare, belligerence creeping into his eyes, "Life moves on".

Moved by instinct, Farrah reached out to touch the

man's shoulder. Though he did not move, a momentary shock flickered over his face as if he had been struck.

"Please, won't you join us?" She asked.

Devin inclined his head and sat, a hardness, more in keeping with his features, chasing the look of embarrassment from his face.

I cannot say what they saw in Devin initially that drew them to him. His animosity and lack of judgement when roused to ire (a frequent occurrence, I admit) had ensured his isolation for years. Yet, with increasing regularity, they found themselves sharing a table with him in the inn taproom and inviting him along on their outings to the marketplace. Perhaps they saw past the hard anger he draped around himself to the pain within, then perhaps deeper still to the true self beneath it all. Devin held this part of him deep within his being, a faint, flickering light that told of magnificent strength and compassion all but forgotten to himself. Pain had stolen the joy that was once his, replacing it with a quick-rising ferocity and a general distrust of his fellow man.

I do not know, either, what drew Devin to the four of them. Perhaps he recognised them as fellow sufferers—people too fractured to judge his faults, for his growing loyalty to them was far more than the fulfilment of a debt. One evening, as they all sat in comfortable silence in the inn's taproom, he looked up from his drink and said, "This would've made my wife 'appy, seeing me with people like this."

Dahlia smiled gently, "What was her name?"

Devin's countenance lightened somewhat, "Cymbeline."

Adam stifled a laugh, "Cymbeline? But that is a man's name!"

"She was born Agnes but changed it as soon as she could. She always liked the name, said Shakespeare made a mistake making Cymbeline a man." Now he did smile, "She was funny like that." He paused a moment before continuing, "Don't know what she saw in me, really. She always said there was goodness there, but she was wrong. She made me good, made me believe I was someone better than I am. When she died…" he trailed off, the sweetness of the past fading in the face of the bitter present. He rallied, "I see 'er sometimes, just 'er face. When the anger comes, it's like a redness, don't really know what I'm doing, but 'er face always stops me, 'olds me back so I don't go too far. So, I know she's still watching, still taking care of me." He trailed off, nodding, then returned his eyes to his cup. It was at that moment that Devin truly became one of them.

I could continue telling of the ensuing months—the happy days when they revelled in their newfound wealth and the joys of being together, and the days when the sorrows of the past seemed poised to overwhelm. It was those days that drove them closer together. Farrah once mentioned to Dahlia, "Sometimes I feel as though we are the most exclusive of groups. Only a bruised and blackened heart will gain one membership." But it was more than the pain that united them as a family, for we all have pain to one degree or another. It was the goodness that resided within them and the hope for lasting joy that they all carried secretly in their hearts.

I understand in writing this to you that the main interest lies in Frayne's extraordinary exploits, which, until this moment, I have barely begun to touch upon. However, I find that, all too often, a hero's heart is lost amidst exaggerations of valour and romantic notions until he is forced into a caricature of himself and lost to the passage of time. The only explanation I can offer for my current approach is that as Frayne's heart is so dear to my own, I cannot write this without attempting to give an accurate representation of it. You must forgive an old lady for her ramblings.

CHAPTER THIRTEEN

Frayne was always restless when it came to thievery. As you may imagine, after relieving two wealthy households of much of their finery, there was little need for any of them to continue seeking out sources of income. However, need does not equate with desire, and since that first day on the quay, Frayne's desire had only grown. It was a self-destructive path that they knew at some level would drive them all to ruin, but so caught up were they in the thrill of their lifestyle and the charisma of Frayne himself that they gladly followed him down it.

That was one of the mysteries of Frayne. He was not as lively or engaging as Adam nor as fiery as Farrah, and he did not possess Dahlia's sweetness or Devin's presence, yet they were all drawn to him. Indeed, any one of them would have sacrificed their lives for him had he asked it. It is so easy to sum each of them up in one word, but when it comes to Frayne I am hopelessly lost.

Having turned his back on house robbing, Frayne

sought adventure in a new vein of thievery. As always, Adam was the first to hear of his idea. They were sitting on the roof of the inn, watching the feeble rays of sunlight fight to make their way above the horizon and penetrate through the haze of morning fog. They spent many mornings in this manner, reliving the days of their childhoods when they would watch the sunrise from atop a roof each morning.

Frayne glanced over at Adam, "What thinks you of highway robbery, Adam?"

Adam rolled his eyes in mock exasperation, "And what asinine plan of yours would concern highway robbery? I can assure you that if it involves crouching for hours in a damp wood, only to have a hole added to my head by an overenthusiastic lordling, I shall stay home by my fire."

"Have you heard of DuVall?"

Adam laughed, "DuVall? The French gentleman?" with a wave of his hand, he began, "'Here lies DuVall: Reder if male thou art, look to thy purse; if female to thy heart. Much havoc has he made of both; for all men he made to stand, and women he made to fall the second Conqueror of the Norman race, knights to his arm did yield, and ladies to his face. Old Tyburn's glory; England's illustrious Thief, Du Vall, the ladies' joy; Du Vall, the ladies' grief.' I stood there, Frayne, stood in Saint Paul's, and read those words. A lovely bit of poetry inspired by two indispensable words, 'here lies'. That is all that highway robbery will get you—a few words on a scrap of stone, an old rope necklace, and a pretty view from the top of a tree. Men like DuVall, the only glory they receive is in legends."

Frayne smiled, "That is all the glory any of us will receive, Adam."

"There is no more merit in highway robbery than in any other type of thievery. If anything, the wages are less than we are accustomed to."

"There is a certain glamorous grandeur to the profession that DuVall was responsible for adding. I will not believe that, if you truly stood in Saint Paul's, you did not feel any desire to follow in his footsteps. 'Old Tyburn's glory; England's illustrious Thief…the ladies' joy'."

Adam sighed, his air resigned, "Well, one would never wish to deprive a lady of joy." He grinned, "Adam and Frayne, gentlemen of the road, if not for the money, then for the glory and a nice bit of posey on a scrap of stone at the end." Adam never could refuse Frayne.

It so happened that Devin caught wind of their plans. It was no great surprise, as the man now spent all his spare time in the company of at least one of the four. The introduction of his presence was gradual but gladly received. He doted upon Farrah and Dahlia like a father would his daughters. Though he was by no means old enough to be their father, his carefully lined face and hardened air lent him an age greater than his own. Neither woman remembered her father, and perhaps sensing his grief at the loss of his family, they readily gathered that singular man into their hearts. Adam and Frayne were perhaps less ardent in their approach but quickly considered him no less than a friend and a co-conspirator, for Devin soon made it apparent that he was no friend of the law.

While Frayne and Adam tried to take a subtle approach to crime, Devin's history proved that his methods were brasher. His wife's serene influence had calmed him greatly, but upon her death, he was undone, and the rage that had lain dormant within him was released. Over time, they learned of past brawls, disturbances, threats, and thefts. Perhaps such a man should have unnerved them, but they recognised that much of his rage was spent, and once again, deep within himself, he longed for peace.

So, with Devin included in their number, preparations began. Adam and Frayne had conjured up an image of the highway gentleman they wished to create. It was a fanciful figure, a combination of romantic danger and mystery infused with all the practicality both could muster, which is to say very little. However foolish it may sound on paper, they were young enough to dream of it, and the rest eager enough to follow.

They began with horses. Frayne insisted that they purchase three of the finest in various pale shades, and he rented a private stable just outside of the city for them to stay in. It was an extravagant move and perhaps overcautious, but their purses allowed for it with little complaint. Of course, his highwayman would be a gentleman, requiring a fine horse and all the accoutrements befitting such a station. However, even in the city horses could be easily identified, so for prudence's sake, a different horse would be used each night, its colour disguised by a layer of charcoal.

The next step, and perhaps the one that brought the most enjoyment, was dressing the highwayman. Adam took to the task with his usual flair. Standing in the middle of the room where they were all gathered, he struck a dramatic pose. "Such a man must be clothed in his finest each evening, and only the darkest shades of ebony shall suffice! He must have a mask, a hat with a dapper plume, and fine boots! Of course, there must be a flashing rapier, a gleaming pistol, and a concealed dagger. He shall be a man to rival men, and all ladies shall swoon at the sight of him!" He winked at Dahlia, who playfully rolled her eyes.

The inn where they had first stayed had become something of their home. The innkeeper paid them little notice, provided they settled their rent in a timely manner.

Each day, they gathered around a small table in Frayne's upstairs room to discuss plans and methods.

"If until this point I have failed to make my position quite clear," Adam stated, "I shall make it clear now. I refuse to squander night after night, crouching in the dirt awaiting the passing of some fine gentleman who shall make such efforts worth my while." He laughed, "As though I were some romantic fool awaiting rescue from my squalor."

"I agree with Adam." Frayne nodded, "Our time would be better spent watching the roads and seeking out news of wealthy travelling gentlemen."

"And what excuse shall we provide for asking after the affairs of such men?" Farrah inserted, "If we continuously inquire after a man, then a few days later he is robbed, our faces will be the first to appear on wanted notices. After the disastrous conclusion of our last endeavour, surely we would be wise to begin this one with greater care?"

"Of course, I understand your concern," Frayne made a placating gesture, "but thievery entails a certain degree of boldness and prior preparation. Waiting in the undergrowth and jumping out at each passing carriage, unaware of any weapons their occupants may be carrying, would prove more foolhardy than making enquiries."

"Well, I think that wandering around, prying into the travel habits of gentlemen, is extremely foolish. You may as well admit that you are afraid of dirtying your coat, or perhaps you care little if we are all betrayed and jailed."

Farrah knew her claims were absurd even as she made them, but some fear still lingered in her heart, tied to the memory of the cold stone cell. And perhaps, deep within herself, she had not entirely forgiven Frayne for allowing her to end up in that cell in the first place.

Frayne's usually placid visage was turning a heated

shade of red.

Adam laughed and turned to Frayne, "'Dispute not with her: she is lunatic.'"

Now it was Farrah's face that reddened, but her angry response was forestalled by a muffled clatter that sounded just outside their door. They all hesitated, and Dahlia made a slight movement towards the window.

Their silence was broken by Devin's angry whisper, "Bleeding innkeepers. 'Ave to 'ave their ear to every bleeding keyhole they can find."

His mutinous advance on the door was checked by a firm hand on his shoulder. Frayne, his expression calm once more, motioned him back to his chair, then strode easily forward and opened the door sharply, startling the figure crouching behind it.

A little brown head lifted to reveal a small face and a guilty expression, caught in the motion of bending to the floorboards. Neat little hands were frozen in the act of reaching for the small wooden doll who seemed to be the cause of the disturbance. Adam laughed in relief.

Frayne immediately dipped into a courteous bow, retrieved the doll, and presented it, with a flourish, to the little girl. "Your child, Madam."

She met his gaze with a defiant glare but took the toy gently from his proffered hand. "Thank you" she sniffed impetuously. If the girl was embarrassed at being discovered in such a compromising position, she gave no hint to it.

"May I inquire after your name, Madam?"

"Bessie." a hint of uncertainty.

"Bessie, a name well-fitting for such a beautiful lady. Do you live here, Bessie?"

His outrageous flattery evoked a smile and a toss of her head. "Yes, my father owns this inn." More than a touch of pride now coloured her small voice.

"Ah, so you are an heiress. And a charming heiress at that! I am delighted to make your acquaintance." Another sweeping bow. How could the child not grin?

"And I, you. May I inquire after your name, Sir?" The words were carefully pronounced.

"Frayne, Madam."

"Frayne, I am delighted." And with a quick bob and a mischievous grin, she ran, clutching her doll to her chest.

Laughter erupted as Frayne closed the door.

"What a singular child." Dahlia smiled at the amused expression on Devin's face.

"I like her," Frayne announced, returning to the table.

"Of course you do. You have a fancy for imperious women." Adam cast a sly glance at Farrah who was watching Frayne, a half-smile on her lips. Adam snorted, "Besotted," then in a falsetto, "'I am bewitched with the rogue's company. If the rascal have not given me medicines to make me love him, I'll be hanged.'"

Farrah scowled, but laughter won over, "That is absurd!"

Adam winked at Frayne, "'The lady doth protest too much, methinks.'"

Farrah grinned and rolled her eyes. "To return to matters of import, having considered Frayne's position, perhaps you are right. I did not contemplate the possibility of an armed or guarded carriage."

Frayne nodded, "Then we agree. We shall begin searching for an appropriate target immediately."

There was little else to plan, for what more is required of a highwayman than to ride up to a passing carriage, flourish his pistols, and relieve the flustered occupants of their belongings? Nevertheless, Adam and Frayne spent weeks debating location, targets, weaponry, and countless other details that later seemed so inconsequential. The five of them spent their days traversing the main roads into and out of the city, inspecting travellers, guards, and locations where the trees grew thick by the side of the road.

After much inspection and debate, they decided upon their first target—a middle-aged gentleman who reached the city early each morning and left after dark each night. From what information they gleaned, they ascertained that he was moderately wealthy and had frequent dealings with other gentlemen in the city—yet loathed the noise and bustle of urban life, preferring instead to settle in the country and risk the dangers of the road each day. Such men rarely travelled with more than a parcel of inconsequential documents and a purse, but his predictability appealed to Farrah's desire for caution.

I shall pass over the details of the day itself (as the final preparations hardly make for interesting reading) to the night. Much to Adam's consternation, the five would-be-highwaymen found themselves crouched for hours amongst the trees awaiting their belated gentleman. When the sound of approaching carriage horses finally signalled his arrival, Devin was the first to emerge from the undergrowth swathed all in black, bestriding the charcoal-covered mare they had brought along.

They had all concurred that Devin's intimidating air made him the ideal candidate to approach the gentleman in the carriage. Meanwhile, Adam and Farrah would seize the reins of the carriage horses and hold the driver at gunpoint while Frayne and Dahlia watched, with guns drawn, from the rear to ensure that no other traveller would take them by surprise. It was an adequate plan, but unfortunately, it failed spectacularly upon execution.

The gentleman in question was of a nervous disposition and was prone to losing his wits upon provocation. Finding himself faced with a hulking phantom, rather than turn over his purse and be safely on his way, the man drew his pistol and with shaking hands, fired upon Devin. Of course, any true highwayman would have put a bullet through the gentleman's head the moment the weapon was drawn, but Devin had little desire to harm the quaking man. Indeed, up until the moment the bullet grazed his arm, Devin had not believed that anyone in the gentleman's position would be foolish enough to attempt retaliation.

Upon hearing the shot, the driver came to the immediate conclusion that his master had been killed and his life was now forfeit. Fear also revealed him to be a man of little prudence, for moments after the shot rang out, the driver whipped his horses, and they took off into a frenzied gallop, knocking Adam and Farrah to the ground. Adam's pistol discharged as he fell, grazing one of the carriage horses and narrowly missing the fortunate driver, who rattled away from them as though the Devil himself was in pursuit.

Frayne and Dahlia immediately ran to assist Adam and Farrah while Devin staggered across the road, clutching his arm and hurling curses at the fast-receding carriage.

"What happened?" Frayne demanded.

"Bleeding sod 'ad a bleeding gun. He just took it out and shot my bleeding arm. I'll kill that bleeding idiot!" And for a moment it did seem as though Devin would take after the carriage, but an instant later, he sat down heavily upon the road, his head between his knees.

CHAPTER FOURTEEN

Back at the inn, Farrah tended to Devin's arm, wincing as her own abrasions were disturbed, while Frayne and Adam discussed the evening's events heatedly. Dahlia quietly excused herself to return to her shop, and once Devin was sufficiently bandaged, Farrah followed her there, leaving the men alone to scheme. She wandered through the darkened streets, paying no heed to the direction she took—the way to Dahlia's home was as familiar to her feet as the shoes she wore. She tapped lightly upon the shop door before entering, trusting that Dahlia would know it was her. Although Farrah rented a room at the inn and spent all her days there, most nights found her walking through the dark streets to spend her nights in the small spare bed in the rooms behind the shop.

The two had first met as children at the workhouse, though Farrah had spent many lonely years there before Dahlia had arrived. Dahlia was a wraith of a girl, blanched with a pinched face that enhanced the bulbous quality of her pale eyes. Long, dark hair hung in tatters around her slight frame. To see her then, a pathetic figure fading into the background, none would have guessed at the beauty that she would grow to possess.

It was months after her arrival that Dahlia finally worked up the courage to speak to Farrah. The younger girl had long admired Farrah's resilience of spirit; while many of the other children lived with heads bent, eyes glazed, Farrah moved through her desolate world with strength emanating from her very being. It was not the sullen, resentful anger that inspired some children to displays of defiant rebellion. It was deeper, stronger, beautiful. It was the fire of Mrs Alves within her.

Farrah took Dahlia under her wing, not from a sense of pity but from the innate knowledge that she needed Dahlia every bit as much as Dahlia needed her. The two became as close as sisters, and it seemed as though the fire within Farrah reignited some of the sparks that had once burned within Dahlia. Neither of the girls spoke of their lives before the workhouse. Farrah found that the joys of the past were rendered painful in the face of the bitter present, so she kept them carefully locked away—a small, tender brightness in the recesses of her heart. She never did discover a great deal regarding Dahlia's past; even when Dahlia left her wretched childhood behind her, she rarely spoke of the days before she knew Farrah, and Farrah did not inquire. It was evident enough that the young girl had been broken long before she entered the workhouse. I wonder now if perhaps Dahlia had forgotten much of her own past. Our minds know how much pain we can tolerate and gracefully shut away that which is too much for us to bear.

The most steadfast bonds are forged through trials, and Farrah and Dahlia were soon inseparable. The girls found their friendship most comforting at night when the darkness came to steal what little light was fostered within their hearts during the day. Farrah would awaken, tears staining her cheeks, with a vague recollection of having called out for her mother, or sometimes Frayne, to find Dahlia beside her, soothing her, calming her, until sleep claimed them both. And each night, Dahlia would awake, silent and trembling, having faced some nameless horror. Then Farrah would hold the small girl tightly against her chest and rock her, just as Mrs Alves had once held Farrah when the night's terrors had proved too much to bear.

When they left the workhouse, the two remained together. They fashioned a new life for themselves as far from the discomforts of their childhoods that their limited means could take them. When they met Frayne and Adam, it seemed that the bleakness of their past was behind them, washed away by the thrilling adventure of the present. The darkness that had come stealing in with the night for so long seemed to lose interest in them as the light fostered by the day became too great for it to overcome. Still, there were nights when it came to them, almost curiously, worming into their hearts, sifting through the black memories that lay in the shadowy corners of their minds.

That evening, when Dahlia heard the crack of a pistol and saw Adam and Farrah scrambling to escape the plunging hooves of the carriage horses, she knew that the darkness was watching. She knew that in her dreams that night, she would see the hooves come down with painful accuracy and see the trembling pistol snatch away the life of not only Devin but Frayne as well. She would be left alone, trembling, surrounded by the empty husks of everyone she loved, while the darkness smiled lazily and marked down another success. So, she was unsurprised when Farrah stole into her room. It was their room, really. Two beds stood side by side, separated by a small table, with a large trunk at the bottom of each bed.

Farrah smiled, "They are well, all of them. Devin's arm was merely grazed, we have nothing to fear."

Dahlia smiled back and nodded, but that night, she awoke trembling, Farrah holding her, as burning tears traced all too familiar patterns down her face.

While Devin slept, Adam and Frayne sat hunched over a table, discussing how they could have avoided the evening's disaster.

Adam shook his head. "We could not have known that the fellow had a gun."

"Yet we should have assumed it. You have always said, "'Tis best to weigh the enemy more mighty than he seems'. We should not have relied upon good fortune to ensure that he would be unarmed and incapable of defending himself."

"To reply to Shakespeare with Shakespeare, 'What's done cannot be undone'."

"No, but the mistakes of the past can be avoided in the future. I could have got you killed tonight, Adam. You, Farrah, and Devin. Truthfully, when you were knocked down, I thought you were gone."

"'S not your responsibility, Mate. If we die doing this, 's by our own choice, we all know the risk we take."

"Then why is it that I feel so responsible?"

Adam laughed bitterly, "Because you have lost everyone and everything you have ever cared about. You did not know the father you both despise and long to emulate. You were given Trudy for a mother, a vicious, wanton hag, and deprived of the only woman who ever loved you the way that a mother should love her child. Even Farrah was taken from you, and because you were a child, you find the fault, not in the ones who truly hurt you, not in fate, not in God nor the Devil, or the arbitrary cruelty of the world, but in yourself. So, you take the guilt of the world upon your shoulders. You accept the condemnation that should be apportioned to chance and allow it to plague you. You believe you are destined to lose all you care about in one manner or another and that it is you, and only you, who is to blame for that loss. And throughout it all, a twisted part deep within you whispers that you deserve all the pain that comes for some apparent crime known only to yourself. You deserve it."

Adam shook his head and gritted his teeth, "Whatever that voice says, whatever accusations the darkness whispers into your mind, do not believe its lies. Someone," his voice came near to breaking, and he faltered, "someone once told me, 'When the darkness comes, when the pain of life seems too great to bear, look for the light, fix your eyes upon it, and have hope that this too shall pass.'" He smiled at a memory and whispered, "'For it is hope that carries us onwards.'"

Frayne gazed at him for a long time, surprise mingling with the various emotions flickering across his face. "You are eloquent, Adam, even without the words of Shakespeare."

Adam shook off the melancholy of the past, "Nah, just all too familiar with pain."

They sat for a while in contemplative silence, and then Adam grinned with a sudden idea. "I think, perhaps, what needs to happen is we need to make them too afraid to fight back."

Frayne nodded in comprehension, "A man may fight another man to defend his purse, but what man will fight a spirit to defend the same object?"

A sly look entered Adam's eyes, "And what spirit does man fear the most but the Devil? After all, we are gentlemen, and Shakespeare said, 'The Prince of Darkness is a gentleman'."

Frayne pondered this, "Nevertheless, perhaps it would be in the interest of wisdom to have Farrah and Dahlia remain behind, at least until we are sure that the danger has passed."

Adam readily nodded his assent. For one to die in such an endeavour seemed somewhat dramatic and glorious, yet to send the woman you loved into such danger was foolhardy in the extreme.

They announced their decision to Farrah and Dahlia the next morning. What had seemed to be a noble and prudent notion the night before began to seem somewhat bigoted when facing the women. Devin, enjoying his lunch in the taproom, watched in amazement as the ordinarily even-tempered Dahlia stormed downstairs and out of the inn while Adam, red-faced and scowling, dropped into a chair next to him.

"You've been chasing one of the barmaids then?" Devin asked.

Adam sputtered in protest, scowled deeper, and then made to chase after Dahlia. He was forestalled by Frayne sitting down heavily at the table as Farrah followed Dahlia outside, allowing the door to close behind her more audibly than was necessary.

Farrah found Dahlia in the stables, rinsing away the layer of charcoal that they had applied to one of the horses the night before. Farrah joined her, and soon they were covered in speckles of black water. Grey streaks adorned Dahlia's face, where she had attempted to wipe away angry tears. After about ten minutes, she spoke, "Adam told me, as cavalierly as anything, that I must stay here! As though I am some timid woman to sit calmly by the fire while he flies off to get himself killed!" She took a shuddering breath, "I swear, when Death comes for Adam, he will dance a merry jig, quote some of his infernal Shakespeare, and rush off to shake Lucifer's hand, with no mind if he leaves me weeping and wailing and cursing the Devil. Well, the Devil take him then! The Devil take them all!" She paused, shaking with silent sobs, then gained mastery of herself. "I am sorry, Farrah, you know that I think the utmost of Frayne, but they speak of long life and undying love, yet we both know that they will not grow to be old men."

Farrah nodded, "And neither would have it any other way." She sighed, "Do not doubt for a moment, Dahlia, that it kills me knowing that, but I would not try to change it. This mad desire for adventure is as much a part of Frayne and Adam, too, as his limbs and danger is a necessary part of that adventure. It is what drives Frayne—remove it, and he will be but a shadow of himself." She laughed, "That is what I ought to say, I know, but Frayne also told me I must stay here. They are fools to think we would be content to remain behind, shaking and fretting, yet doing our womanly duty and remaining home. I love Frayne with all my heart, yet sometimes…" She did not finish her thought aloud, but either man would have quailed under her expression.

Dahlia nodded in grateful assent.

Farrah continued, "I have already decided that I shall accompany them whether they wish it or not, and since they do not desire my presence, they shall not see me unless absolutely necessary. Will you join me?" She knew she need not have asked.

When night fell, three men dressed all in black left the inn on foot. Ten minutes later, two hooded figures slipped from the inn and began to follow the men's progress out of the city.

CHAPTER FIFTEEN

Adam shivered despite his cloak and let out a long stream of curses under his breath.

Frayne chuckled softly, "One would imagine you would be accustomed to the cold after the childhood we endured."

Adam scowled, "It is precisely because of that childhood that I revile the cold, especially a damp cold such as this." He paused and checked his fingertips for feeling, "Do you think they will come?"

"Undoubtedly." Frayne's voice held a note of disappointment.

Devin, who had remained silent for the past hour, huffed, then startled at a slight rustling in the undergrowth to his right.

Adam grinned at him, "'Suspicion always haunts the guilty mind; the thief doth fear each bush an officer.'"

Frayne signalled for him to be silent, then smiled with relief. "Our wait is over. Farrah and Dahlia, please join us. Dignified women do not lurk in forests."

The two emerged with damp leaves and briars adorning their cloaks.

Dahlia glared at them, "You have passed the last hour awaiting us?"

Adam stretched, "Unfortunately. We are all too familiar with your stubborn temperaments. If you are going to join us regardless of what we urge you, you may as well aid us productively rather than crouching amongst the trees with kitchen knives." He glanced disdainfully at the small weapons they had attempted to conceal in their hands.

Farrah seethed. They were all irritable after an uncomfortable and somewhat disappointing evening, "You are fools, all of you."

Adam turned to her mildly, "'Teach not thy lip such scorn, for it was made for kissing, lady, not for such contempt.'"

Both women looked ready to fly at him then.

Devin shook his head, "Don't matter. They're 'ere, we're 'ere, now let's get out of these blasted woods. No one's coming down this road tonight."

Admittedly, their tempers all improved once they were back in front of the small fire that warmed Frayne's upstairs room. After each had apologised profusely to the rest, Adam and Frayne began to lay out their latest plan.

When they finished, Devin laughed in surprise, "Seems to me it would just be easier to hold them at gunpoint, tie the driver to the wheel, take the money, and leave."

Adam nodded, "Certainly, it would be easier. However, it is not for the ease or the money that we steal, but for the glory."

Devin just stared, "But this is madness!"

Watching Frayne's eyes take on a new and vivid life as he contemplated his current idea, it occurred to Farrah for the first time that perhaps, residing in him was a kind of madness. It was certainly plausible that his childhood on the streets had instilled a kind of controlled insanity within him that found its fruition in his dramatically complex schemes. However, considering the rest of the group, if there was any lunacy, it resided in them all, with Frayne being perhaps the sanest among them. She shook off the thought. "Devin, when we steal, it is for the thrill of accomplishment and ingenuity. Few things are more beautiful than seeing a dramatic, hopelessly impossible plan through to completion. And this plan," she laughed, "is brilliant in its madness."

Frayne's plan played out spectacularly. He and Devin spent an afternoon in the woods, partially cutting through a thick tree that grew on the very edge of the road. When they were certain it could be felled by a few brief strokes of an axe, they doused as much of the trunk as they could reach in a foul-smelling, flammable liquid. Meanwhile, Adam had finished purchasing two more fine horses and proceeded to coat all five of their beasts in a charcoal mixture. Farrah and Dahlia remained at Dahlia's shop, finishing five identical outfits from bolts of black cloth.

When the outfits were complete, Dahlia produced five enormous feathers, dyed deep ebony, from a bag, "Adam insisted that our highwayman should have 'a hat with the most dapper of plumes'." she laughed, "These may be too large to be dapper, but that will only increase the fun of it all, to see the three of them parading around, waving their feathers like ostriches."

Farrah smiled good-naturedly, "And it serves them right for all the trouble they have caused us!"

Night found the five of them waiting at the edges of the forest, dressed in identical black outfits, masks obscuring their features, each leading a horse the same dark colour as the rest. Frayne and Devin remained by the tree while the rest stood further down the road. Adam swatted irritably at the large feather in his hat. It had come loose from its holdings and was dancing around his face. He paused, hand raised, "It is coming". Within moments, the sound of hooves heralded the approaching carriage. He mounted his horse and turned to see Farrah and Dahlia doing the same. He almost shook with excitement, "Any moment, any moment now. There!" As the carriage passed them, a tree fell across the road, directly in its path, causing the driver to pull sharply on the reins to avoid a disastrous collision.

No sooner had he stopped than flames leapt across the bark, engulfing the whole tree within seconds. His horses screamed, their eyes rolling, and the carriage began to move backwards.

"Now, now!" Adam cried, and the three of them emerged from the undergrowth to surround the rear and sides of the carriage while Frayne and Devin appeared at the front to face the driver.

The five began circling the coach, none of them speaking, their horses' hooves wrapped in thick dark cloths to muffle any sound. The burning tree cast flickering shadows that seemed to wrap themselves around the riders, making it difficult to tell the difference between man and shade. The sounds of burning wood twined with the screams of the carriage horses into a kind of music that the terrified driver chanted along to, his prayers and breathless pleading running together until all that was discernible was one line, repeated over and over, "Yea, though I walk through the valley of the shadow of death, I will fear no evil."

Much to their relief, the man produced no weapon. Even if he had, his trembling was too great to make any use of it. Finally, they stopped. Adam and Devin each produced a blade and levelled them at the driver. Frayne leaned down from his horse, placed a gloved hand upon the door handle, and opened it to reveal two men and a woman cowering in the carriage. What a sight they beheld! It is no wonder to me that the woman fainted dead away when she saw the figure framed in the doorway. How easily I can picture it—Frayne, swathed and masked in black, a pistol in one hand and his reins in the other, lit only by the dim light from the carriage and the roaring fire behind him, smoke rolling through the air and the unholy cacophony of man, beast, and flame, singing of the misfortune that had fallen upon these poor souls.

A long-ago memory flickered to the forefront of Frayne's mind of a cold doorway and two figures stalking him in the night. He smiled, and it was no human smile.

"What we want," his low voice was a purr, "is your money or your life."

Within moments, the two men had torn all objects of value from their persons and offered them, with shaking hands, to Frayne. He took them, then cast a disdainful glance at the woman, still lying senseless upon the carriage floor. It would take too much effort to remove the jewels from around her neck, and the burning tree was already beginning to extinguish. He signalled to Adam, and the five of them melted away into the forest, the dying flames allowing the darkness to encroach, disguising their retreat. Fifteen minutes passed before the driver, gaining mastery of himself once more, was able to turn the carriage and hurtle away from the cursed place in the direction that he had first come.

Two weeks later, an interesting development occurred. Adam was wandering through the marketplace when he recognised that poor man. The driver leaned against a stall, talking to its minder, while a small crowd gathered about him. Around his neck hung a large, roughly hewn wooden cross, and in his hand, he clutched what appeared to be a page of scripture. Adam sidled closer to hear what the man was saying.

"...then they called up fires from Hell so we couldn't pass, and the demons descended upon us, possessed the horses, and struck me down with weakness. Then Beelzebub himself came out of the flames, and for the noblemen's greed, he took all their wealth and put a blight upon their souls. As for the lady, he struck her down with his fearsome gaze."

A murmur swept through the crowd. "What'd the demons look like?" the stallholder asked.

The driver widened his eyes and swept his arms about, "They were dressed in shadows! When they drew their swords, they were made of flames, and writhing on their hats were the souls of damned spirits!"

Adam smirked Dahlia's feathers had been worth the discomfort of wearing them.

But the man was not finished. Encouraged by his enraptured audience, he continued, "There were at least twenty of them, all eight feet tall and riding black, monstrous horses whose hooves didn't touch the ground, for they made no noise when they moved!"

Still smirking, Adam returned to the inn and reported the driver's words to the rest. Frayne was delighted, and for their next theft, he had cushions strapped to their saddles so that when they sat upon them, they truly did appear inhumanly tall.

For well over a year, the five of them pursued highway robbery. Frayne altered the locations and details of the ambushes, but the concept remained unchanged. By unspoken consent, it was typically Frayne who approached the occupants of a carriage. Most memorable was the evening when the five found themselves intercepting a carriage carrying four young duchesses away from a night of revelry in the city. As Frayne leaned into the carriage to accept a handful of necklaces, one of the brazen wretches grabbed him and kissed him full on the mouth. Farrah had been waiting close by, and when Frayne pulled back in surprise, she took his place in the open doorway, leaned towards the offending woman, and with a sharp rap with the butt of her pistol, rendered her unconscious. From that moment on, they agreed to rotate roles.

One night, Devin took the lead. The sweet man, noticing the distress of the waylaid women he faced, put aside his pistols and graciously accepted their purses with a bow to each, leaving them with their jewels still fastened securely about their necks. Adam was livid when he heard of the riches Devin had passed over, but the event merely insinuated Devin more firmly into the hearts of Dahlia and Farrah.

CHAPTER SIXTEEN

Mr Simmons, it is no secret the wealthy are loathed by their less fortunate countrymen. Such is the way of the world. For hundreds of years, the populace has glorified those audacious few who dared to snub their noses at the scornful affluent and their pet officers. I speak not of the children who rob gentlemen of a few coins, nor of the nameless men who lurk in the darkest corners of cities; I speak of the glorified legends who have joined the ranks of demigods because of the people's desire for a hero.

Legends such as Robin of Sherwood and Claude DuVall begin as men. Their flaws are softened, their escapades heightened, their romances made beautiful and tragic until the man is lost to time. Before long, the fancy is secured in the populace's imagination to be passed on, forever reinvented, to become what the people of the day need.

In Frayne's day, these fancies were at a height. The people had long become disillusioned and malcontent. The Faerie Queene's reign had long ended, and the fickle populace longed to return to those golden days. In the city, every hindrance or humiliation of a lawkeeper was praised. Everywhere, stories of gallant thieves and gentlemen of the road were dreamed up and sold for pennies apiece. The people wanted a hero, but they made do with Frayne.

The driver's story spread like the plague, infecting people's minds and making them shake with the fear and the thrill of it. As Frayne continued to stalk the roads leading to the city, the rumours increased, some, I imagine, spread by Frayne himself. Quickly, the rumours changed to stories, and the truth of the events was lost somewhere beneath the layers of romanticised drama. Frayne was a demon, nameless, faceless, with powers beyond mortal understanding, sent by God and the Devil to torment the rich. Or he was a man, once wealthy, who sought revenge upon the upper echelons of society for murdering a beautiful peasant girl that he had loved. Or he was King Arthur, alive again, seeking to galvanise the people and lead them to victory against the blighted government that claimed hold of the land.

His robberies were exaggerated with each telling. He stole fifty pounds, six hundred pounds, eight thousand pounds. He left sixty women without jewels, one hundred men without purses, and impoverished several minor lords. He had anywhere between four and fifty followers and hundreds of horses. He was the rich man's terror, but he did not hurt or kill, and the people declared him a hero.

Such idols are considered dangerous to society, and it was not long before posters calling for his arrest appeared—yet without a name or a face to accompany them, they posed little threat to Frayne. In defiance of these posters, poems and letters began to appear, pinned up on doors, market stalls, and landmarks. They praised the actions of the highwayman, defied the government's men, and, in some cases, even asked for assistance. It was the last of these that caused the most contention amongst the five highwaymen. One letter, in particular, caught their attention. It was written by an older woman who lived on the outskirts of the city. It read:

> Man of the road
> I beg you save my boy from prison where he is kept for stealing six coins to feed me, his mother. He is but twelve years old and the only family I have.

Adam carried it into the busy taproom one afternoon with a grin on his face. "This letter first appeared three days ago, and the word is that the guard around the prison has already doubled!"

Frayne frowned, "But why would they assume that we would attempt to rescue the boy? We are highwaymen. As far as anyone knows, we have never had anything to do with prisons."

Adam's grin did not falter, "They assume because we are heroes to the people, and the men at the prison fear us."

Frayne shook his head, "We are not heroes, Adam. I am not a hero. We steal, we threaten, and we terrify. And in the past, we have hurt. There is nothing about that to suggest that we are gallant men."

"You said it yourself, Frayne, when you spoke to me of DuVall. We do this for glory, and with glory comes expectations."

"But expectations may go unfulfilled."

Farrah, who had been listening, joined the conversation, "You give the people excitement, Frayne, and hope."

He rounded on her sharply, "I am not here to bring hope! Do you think that I have not also heard the poems and stories that are circulating about us? Some are amusing, and indeed, some aid us, but I have heard a few call us the Liberator, come to tear down the rich and powerful. There are enough malcontents in this city, all looking for a leader, but I tell you now, I have no political agenda. My name shall not become a rallying cry, and if any of you wish otherwise, you may leave."

The four stared at him in silence for a while, then Dahlia placed a consoling hand upon his arm, "Frayne, we all steal for the sake of stealing. There is no other agenda behind this. We think only of the boy and the satisfaction of abducting someone so closely guarded. Imagine it—locked doors, double the guard, and he would just disappear."

Frayne smiled wanly, "You realise all of you, there shall be no reward in this? The boy's mother is unlikely to pay us."

Devin looked unsure, but Adam smiled, "Our reward shall be the thrill of accomplishment and the glory of achieving the impossible, 'What's past is prologue'!" And in that short time, it was decided.

Later, they gathered in their rented room at the inn.

"Perhaps it would be best, considering the circumstances, to refrain from overcomplicating this theft," Frayne suggested.

Devin sighed in relief at his words.

"The last rescue attempt went rather well." Farrah added, "Could we not replicate that?"

Adam shook his head, "Last time, we had the good fortune of knowing that your cell had an outward-facing window. We have no idea where the boy is being held."

"But surely, for such a petty crime, he will be in the same temporary holding cell that Farrah was in?" Dahlia said.

Frayne shook his head, "With Farrah, we did not have the time to do anything but assume, but with this boy, with the guard doubled and the city's eyes upon us, we should be certain."

Devin nodded, "Aye".

Farrah and Dahlia visited the prison the next day, posing as the boy's aunts. They laughed and chatted with the guards and cooed through a large barred window at the bemused boy. They berated him for his unwashed state, promised to bring him sweets if he behaved, and superciliously passed a file through to him, gesturing at the bars separating his cell from the corridor they stood in.

"He is kept in the Condemned Hole?!" Adam was aghast. "He stole six coins, so they are going to hang him?"

Farrah's face was stern, "He has an old brand upon his hand. This is not the first time they have caught him stealing."

Adam shook his head, "Poor little sod. That could have been me growing up. There are too many desperate fools in this world."

"At least we can be of aid to one of them." Dahlia smiled gently, "He did look a pathetic figure. His mother will be glad to have him returned."

"As to that matter," Frayne said, "did you manage to pass him the file?"

Dahlia nodded.

"And he knows how to use it?"

"We explained to him the best we could." Farrah said, "But we were wary of the guards and did not want to remain too long. He seems resourceful, though, and I trust him to make wise use of it. He was unbound, too, so he should have no trouble."

"Good." Frayne's eyes had taken on the glazed look they always acquired when he was deep in thought.

"Because the boy is kept in the Hole, we will have no opportunity to smuggle him out of an outward-facing window. However, we are fortunate that he is not kept in cuffs or manacles. We shall give him three days to file through one of the iron bars of the grille, and then Farrah and Dahlia shall visit him again."

Farrah strode along the stone corridor, Dahlia beside her. The prison ceilings were lofty, and sunlight streamed through the large window set high in the wall to their right. The summer heat had warmed the entire building, but despite the warmth and the many layers of clothing she wore, Farrah felt cold. Memories of the dark night she had spent there the year before danced through her head. Dahlia seemed to read her thoughts and laid a reassuring hand on her arm. Farrah offered a grateful smile in return, but she could almost hear her heart pounding as they approached the guards. Dahlia strolled towards the guards with her most charming smile adorning her face. Farrah waited until the men seemed sufficiently distracted, then continued past them to the Hole.

The boy gazed out at her—pale eyes terrified in his drawn face.

"Did you get a bar loose?"

He nodded back mutely.

Farrah helped him to pull the bar free, and then laid it by her feet, along with the file that he passed through to her. Then, taking hold of the boy's forearms, she began to pull him through the gap they had made. It was a tight fit, and the boy winced as the stone under him scraped painfully along his meagre stomach. Once he was through, he watched in bewilderment as Farrah began stripping off layers of clothing to reveal another dress beneath. "Here," she thrust the clothes at him, "put these on. And this," she added, extracting a bonnet from beneath her skirts. The boy pulled them over his ragged clothing, his hands shaking every bit as much as hers. While he was dressing, Farrah wedged the iron bar back into place and hid the file in the folds of her cloak. She smiled briefly at the seemingly untouched window, then, grabbing the boy's hand, turned and walked back towards the guards.

Farrah felt her hands grow slick with every step she took. She forced herself to breathe deeply and evenly, relaxing every muscle in her body as she did so, so that within moments, her outward signs of apprehension were gone. She cast her mind back to the last time that she had escaped prison and considered each robbery that she had been an accomplice of since. There had been no terror then, no shaking with trepidation. Why was her response so heightened now? Her answer was Frayne. He seemed to have the unique ability to allay their fears by inspiring so much excitement and confidence within them that everything else was drowned out. She could not determine how he accomplished it—he offered no rousing speeches, practised no galvanising rituals—perhaps it was nothing more than his presence.

In her memory, Frayne had never exhibited any fear, regardless of the dangers they faced together. His quiet self-assurance, originating from somewhere deep inside of him, had a placating effect, while his contagious enthusiasm spurred them on more effectively than any ritual. Perhaps his apathy towards danger should have alarmed her, but as Farrah wiped her hands against her skirts, she thought there were few things she would not give to have him beside her at that moment.

As they approached the guard's table, Farrah was bewildered to notice that it was unmanned. Without pausing to wonder why, she pulled the boy past it and continued out of the prison. It was not until they were walking down the street away from the building that Farrah paused to look back for Dahlia. She did not have to wait long before she saw her hurrying after them. Dahlia reached them, panting slightly from her haste, an amused smile upon her face.

"They all thought to scare me by showing me one of the prisoners. People have been paying silver coins to see him, can you imagine?!" She grew grave, "He is something of a political prisoner, I believe. One of the guards muttered 'rebel', and from what they were hinting at, I think he might have been responsible for some of the pages about Arthur that Adam mentioned." They continued walking, and her voice dropped to a whisper, "They said that he had been tortured for information, and indeed, he was in a fearsome state. They were wrong to believe that it would shock me, though. I have seen far worse."

Farrah nodded grimly in response.

They rounded a corner to find Frayne waiting for them. Though Dahlia and Farrah knew him instantly, to anyone else he would have been unrecognisable. Dirt masked his hair and skin, a patch obscured one eye, and his mouth hung slack, complementing his vacant expression. He grinned at the boy, revealing blackened teeth.

"Leave those clothes on, and run home to your mother, she will be pleased to see you."

The boy gazed at him in awe, then turned and hurried down an alley. Farrah smiled at the boy's expression, then handed Frayne the file, and walked with Dahlia back to the inn.

Meanwhile, Frayne traced their footsteps back towards the prison. He slouched as he went, allowing one foot to drag ever so slightly, giving him a distinctive staggering gait. He entered the prison and went straight to the guards' station. At his request, the men impassively waved him towards the boy's cell. Five minutes later, they stumbled to their feet, roused from their lethargy by the sound of ringing metal and hoarse shouting. They reached the Condemned Hole to find the prisoner missing, and the man who had claimed to be his father vanished. A metal file was left on the ground next to a single iron bar, wrenched free from its hold.

That very day wanted posters appeared all over the city. Some bore a crude sketch of the boy's face, but the rest were adorned with the filthy features of a man who did not exist.

CHAPTER SEVENTEEN

I believe that from the moment the boy's foot touched the paving stones outside the prison door, Death's eye was drawn to Frayne. Everything must, in time, end, and although Frayne's end was still nothing more than a faded smudge on his horizon, the clock was wound, and the hands had begun their slow circuit. After all, once Death's eye is upon you, he will never look away.

The sun had barely crested the horizon when Adam and Frayne left the inn the next day. They strolled through the subdued streets to the marketplace, where listless vendors were beginning to erect their stalls. Like their visits to the inn's roof, this early morning excursion was becoming something of a ritual for the two men. It was reassuring and comforting and tied them to a past that had not yet begun to fade from their memories. They paused occasionally to greet a vendor or to slip into an alleyway to pass coins to the small, familiar ghosts that haunted those dark spaces.

Within the hour, crowds began to form, breaking the

fragile film of stillness left behind by the night. Adam breathed deeply, enjoying the customary smells, and began to hum, as men and women hawked their wares all around him. Frayne smiled at his friend, but a familiar sense of unease was gently pricking at his consciousness. He had learned long ago to listen to that sense, so he abruptly darted into an alleyway, pulling Adam behind him.

"Something is not right."

Adam nodded, then grinned, "We've got a follower. Wondered how long it'd take you to notice."

Frayne scowled at him, "Who?"

Adam jerked his head towards the opening of the alleyway.

The boy that they had liberated the previous day stood some distance from the opening, mouth slightly agape, eyes searching the milling crowds, clearly baffled by their sudden disappearance.

Adam snorted, "Not much use is he?"

He and Frayne slunk together towards the mouth of the alleyway, instinctively hugging the shadowy walls. As one, they leapt out, grabbed the boy's arms, and hauled him back into the privacy of the lane. He squealed and kicked the whole way.

"Don't 'urt me, I swear I ain't got nothin', don't 'urt me!" His eyes rapidly adjusted to the gloom and fastened upon Frayne. He gasped, "It's you, you got me out, you're the Liberator!" His eyes shone with a feverish glow.

Frayne frowned. His disguise had been thorough, and the boy should not have recognised him. He must have followed Farrah and Dahlia back to the inn rather than returning to his mother as they had instructed him.

"What're you doing, Boy?" Adam glowered at him.

"I don't mean no 'arm, I swear. I was just lookin' for you. Me Mum wanted me to say thanks." He paused and shifted his weight back and forth.

Frayne's frown did not abate. The boy bothered him. "And?"

"And…well Sir…I wanted Sir… to come with you, to be an 'ighwayman, Sir, and ride an 'orse and rob toffs, and, and be an 'ero."

Adam laughed, "You don't look much like an 'ero."

"I'll grow, Sir, I'll grow fast, and I'm strong too, Sir."

His expression made Frayne smile. It was something reminiscent of a puppy eager to please its master.

Adam squinted at him, "You ever been on a horse, Boy?"

The boy shook his head mutely, hope and fear painted comically across his face.

Adam glanced at Frayne, who slowly shook his head, a grave expression chasing away his amusement. "We have only just freed you. I will not be the cause of your recapture." He smiled ruefully at the disappointment that stood starkly upon the boy's face.

"Think of your Mum," Adam suggested, placing a hand on his shoulder, "she would never forgive us if something happened to you."

The boy shrugged Adam's hand away, his disappointment turning to bitterness, "I'm old enough to do what I want. Mum won't care, why should you?"

Frayne caught the boy's shoulder and turned him so they stood facing one another, "We care because we know what it is like to have no one watching out for you."

The boy looked to his feet in contrition, "You shouldn't care, Sir, not for me."

Adam smiled and gripped the boy's other shoulder, "It's too late for that, Boy. We're sentimental sods, the both of us."

Frayne grinned at them. Something in the boy's features

and manner reminded him of Adam, "We shall give you two months to prove your reliability. If, during this time, you manage to avoid speaking of us to anyone, we shall reconsider. Do you understand?"

"Yes, Sir, thank you, Sir, thank you kindly."

"And don't get arrested again," Adam added.

"I won't, Sir, I swear." Excitement danced across the boy's face.

Frayne bent over slightly so his eyes were level with the boy's, "Remember, you must tell no one about this, not even your Mum. Yes?"

"Yes, Sir, thank you, Sir, I swear I won't, Sir."

"And what is your name? We cannot keep calling you 'Boy'."

"Christopher, Sir, that's my Christian name, after the saint."

Frayne nodded, "Run home then, Christopher."

"And don't be so obvious next time you follow someone!" Adam called after the boy.

Christopher turned and waved, then disappeared into the teeming crowd.

Adam laughed freely now, "'Nature has framed strange fellows in her time'. Were we ever that eager?"

Frayne grinned, "Do you recall when the barman at the Four Horses offered you half a penny for each glass you could clean?"

Adam nodded soberly, "I washed four, downed the dregs of the remaining glasses, spilt a pail of soapy water over myself, and fell on my arse, but was so eager for those coins that I kept washing anyway."

Frayne shook his head, his shoulders shaking with mirth. "The barkeeper found you sat resolutely on the floor, hiccuping along to your favourite drinking song and rubbing his best glasses on your sodden shirt."

"Bloody man wouldn't even give me my coins, just had you come drag me out."

"And you sang all the way."

Adam smiled, "Good lives we've had, really."

"Few can boast of better."

Frayne and Adam spent the next morning meandering up and down the roads that led to the city, casually taking note of each passing rider and carriage. These excursions were commonplace and allowed them to determine who, out of the frequent passersby, would be best suited to losing their possessions in a highway robbery. As they walked back towards the city for the second time, they noticed a group of six men on horses approaching them. At first, Adam and Frayne took no notice of them, but as the horses came steadily closer, one of the riders began to look vaguely familiar. A few moments later, he was unmistakable. Surrounded by armed men and struggling to remain upon his horse was Christopher.

The boy seemed to recognise them at the same moment, and turning to the men following him, he gestured urgently towards Adam and Frayne.

Adam cursed, "Little sod did a better job of following us this time." A shot rang out, and they both paled, "Bleeding wretch called the guard on us." Adam hissed.

Frayne nodded, "Get off the road. We'll run back to the inn. They might not be able to follow us through the trees."

Together, they broke into a sprint and reached the tree line before the riders had a chance to turn their mounts. For a moment, hope flickered through them, but it quickly fled as the horses, urged on by their masters, left the road and plunged into the trees.

They ran, hearts pounding. Both felt like they were

children on the streets once again, fleeing from an invisible pursuer. Although now the terrain was alien, there were no familiar holes to crouch in or drainpipes to take them far above the reach of their hunters. Hooves crashed through the undergrowth behind them. Another shot cracked the bark of a tree metres to Frayne's left, but the two did not falter. They plunged on and on, deeper into the trees, heading vaguely towards the city. Their only hope of escape was to lose their pursuers in the thickening foliage.

Another shot penetrated a tree next to Frayne's head. He called for Adam to run, then ended his headlong sprint and turned to face the men behind him. There were five, each astride a horse and carrying a pistol, their faces gouged by the merciless branches that they had torn through. Christopher was nowhere in sight. As one, the riders encircled Frayne and lowered their weapons at his heaving chest. One man trotted his horse closer to him, producing a rope as he did so. He smiled a cold, cruel smile, "Stand and deliver." Pain shot through Frayne's head, and darkness claimed him.

Adam fell through the inn's doors into the quiet taproom. He lurched towards a table near the bar, where Farrah and Dahlia were finishing lunch.

Dahlia's eyes widened as she beheld his dishevelled state. "Adam, what…"

"Where's Devin?"

Farrah stood, "He is upstairs. Adam, where is Frayne?"

He seized each woman by the arm, "Upstairs, get upstairs now."

He thrust them towards the back of the taproom. No sooner had they entered the stairway when the door to the inn was flung open once again, and three armed men strode over the threshold, eyeing the few patrons within as they took up positions in front of the bar. One leaned across to the innkeeper, who stood with a glass in one hand and a well-used rag in the other, his face a placid mask.

"We're looking for a man—slight, blonde—and two women. They've been seen around here."

The innkeeper nodded slowly, "The women, one is blonde and one dark-haired?"

The armed man jerked his head in assent.

The innkeeper nodded more vigorously this time, "They were here buying drinks just a few days ago. I'd never seen them before, but they said they'd been staying at an inn by the city wall. Said it was 'far superior in its facilities to this dingy little rat hole'." He sniffed indignantly, "I hope you catch them."

The man scrutinised him for a moment longer, but the innkeeper's face revealed nothing more than a lingering sense of injured pride. The man grunted, gestured to his followers, and left the inn as swiftly as he had entered.

Adam collapsed in relief against the wall of the stairway as he heard the door slam shut. He waited five minutes before venturing back into the taproom, Farrah and Dahlia close behind him. He picked his way gingerly between tables to where the innkeeper still stood, polishing the glass he held.

Adam nodded to him, "Thank you."

The innkeeper shrugged, "Can't stand that kind of man. Besides," he smiled now, "my Bessie is rather attached to your friend. She'd never forgive me if I gave you up."

As if by summons, a small brown head popped up from behind the bar. Bessie grinned, "Where's Frayne?"

CHAPTER EIGHTEEN

Frayne awoke in near darkness. He had dreamed that tiny angry men were dancing upon his skull, and though he was now awake, it felt as though they danced still. Faint moonlight filtered through the small, barred window high up on one wall, illuminating the hard stones on which he lay and a flimsy wooden chair a few metres in front of him. He turned his head to the side and vomited. Moaning quietly, Frayne began pulling himself across the stones towards the chair, being careful not to disturb his head. He crawled no more than a metre before he fell senseless to the floor.

Adam sat with Devin, Farrah, and Dahlia in the back room of Dahlia's shop. He had hastily explained to them all that had occurred with Christopher, then insisted that they remove themselves from the inn.

Adam stood, "I am going to find Frayne, or at least discover what has become of him."

Farrah—pale-faced but resolute—shook her head, "It

is too dangerous, Adam. Frayne would not wish for you to risk yourself on his behalf."

"Yet he would do it for me."

Devin stood also, "I'll go. The man said they're looking for a blonde man and two women. They said nothing about me."

Adam gave a curt nod in response, and Devin quickly slipped out onto the street. He returned an hour later, grim-faced, clutching a page in his hand. He glanced towards Farrah, concern streaking across his face, and then he fixed his eyes upon Adam.

"They've caught 'im it's already been announced." He gestured towards the paper he held.

Adam nodded, "And it was Christopher who betrayed us?"

Dahlia shook her head, "I do not understand. We freed him from prison, we returned him to his mother, and you were going to allow him to join us. He was grateful. Why would he betray Frayne?"

Adam scowled, "'One may smile and smile, and be a villain.'"

Devin continued, "It seems the boy was arrested again when 'e finally went 'ome. There were men waiting for 'im. They gave 'im a choice: 'swing from a rope or give up the man who 'elped you'."

Adam sighed, "He must have followed Farrah and Dahlia to the inn after we freed him. That is how the men found us there today."

"Where is Frayne being held?" Farrah asked.

Devin shifted his weight uneasily, as if unsure how much truth to speak, "'E's imprisoned on the top floor of a temporary 'olding prison." He paused, "'E's been condemned to 'ang first thing Monday."

Adam paled, "'Death is a fearful thing'."

Frayne awoke again in daylight, the pounding in his head reduced to a dull thumping. He lay on the cool floor a few moments longer, assessing each bruised and cramped muscle. For a moment, images from his childhood flickered through his mind—memories of collapsing upon a wooden floor, blood heavy upon his face, bruises staining his skin, and a fear more palpable than any before, tearing into his heart. Then they were gone, the recollections slinking back to the locked place they had escaped from—the darkness hidden once again.

Slowly, he rose to his feet and surveyed the room about him. The chair still stood before him, and now he noticed a bed covered with peculiarly stained sheets resting in one corner. Frayne dragged the chair over to the wall to reach the high window. His heart sank within him. His cell was two stories above the ground—there would be no escape that way. Examining the cell door, he promptly concluded that escape by that means would also prove futile, as it was solidly built and firmly secured.

Frayne assessed the room once more, plans flitting through his mind. He touched his pocket where his captors had failed to remove a small folding razor he kept for emergencies. What manner of fools were these men? The razor would not prove much good against the door or the window. He considered the ceiling. At a glance, it appeared well-made, but it certainly lacked the fortifications placed upon the rest of the room.

Frayne began to determine a course of action. He had no desire to remain in his cell any longer than necessary, so even before the concept had fully formed within his mind, he set to work implementing it. The evening was approaching. Though his cell was high above the ground, the sounds of people passing in the streets below muffled some of the slighter sounds Frayne made. Using his razor, he hewed fiercely at the stretcher of the chair and, in ten minutes, had it free. He returned the dulled blade to his pocket and, placing the stretcher aside, moved the bed into the middle of the room. He climbed onto the bed and gathered his strength, trying to ignore the pain in his head. He paused. The excitement that was coursing through him slowly dulled as other thoughts began to worm their way into his mind. What had become of Adam? The time that Frayne had spent unconscious had seemed fleeting to him, but conceivably, days could have slipped past him unnoticed. If Adam was apprehended, he could well be dead already.

Frayne took a deep breath and began attacking the ceiling with the chair stretcher. He paused again to readjust the bed, then set about his task with a renewed force, grinning as the breach rapidly grew. No inconvenient sensations of guilt or regret for his dishonest life plagued his mind. His brief imprisonment had led to no self-reflection as it had with Farrah. It was not that Frayne had made peace with the illegality of his actions he had simply never had any qualms to begin with. Whether or not his career broached the boundaries of morality did not concern him—his conscience was clear, and his imprisonment nothing more than a minor inconvenience.

The mattress beneath Frayne prevented any noise being made by the rubble he battered away from the ceiling, falling to the floor. However, as he began to push upwards with the piece of wood, he could hear the telltale clattering of tiles and bricks hitting the street below. Moments later, a great shout arose from beyond his window. An unfortunate tailor passing by the prison had been struck upon the head by a tile falling from the rooftop. The initial cry of distress was followed by more. Soon a crowd gathered on the street, calling that the prisoners were escaping. Hearing the clamour, Frayne made a final desperate push, and the last of the tiles gave way and fell to the street, affording him a gap through which he climbed onto the roof.

By this point, night had fallen, and it was no great task to descend unseen to the churchyard below and, from there, scale a low wall to join the crowd gathered at the base of the prison. Flushed with his success and with adrenaline still coursing through him, Frayne gazed intently at the rooftop. He elbowed a large man standing beside him, "There! There! I see him! There is his head, disappearing behind the chimney!" The people around him quickly echoed his shouts. Each onlooker was quite convinced that the shadows of the racing clouds, dancing upon the rooftop, were made by the arm or leg of an escaping convict. Laughing, Frayne moved quickly through the crowd and away into the dark streets.

It did not take Frayne long to reach the inn. Rather than risk recognition by entering through the taproom, he carefully climbed up a drainpipe to his window, which remained unlocked for such an occasion as this. He entered cautiously to find his room deserted and stripped of his belongings. Unperturbed, he nimbly descended via the way he had come and turned instead towards Dahlia's shop.

Frayne had not returned to Dahlia's shop since the day he had followed Farrah there. He quickly became disoriented in the dark and took two wrong turns before finally finding the old building. From where he stood, Frayne could not see any lights within the shop, but he guessed that any lights in the back rooms would be concealed from view of the street. He hesitated, his hand raised to knock. He had entertained the idea that Adam might have been captured along with him, but for the first time, Frayne considered that perhaps the others were also arrested. When he did not find them at the inn, he assumed they had been recognised there and had hidden away in Dahlia's apartments, but now that he was here, he began to doubt himself. With a pervading sense of unease, Frayne retrieved his razor from his pocket and slid it into the gap by the door handle. Quickly, he forced open the door and slipped silently into the deserted shop.

Frayne cautiously felt his way towards the door that led to Dahlia's rooms. A thin ribbon of light stretched across the base, but no sound emanated from beyond it. He drew the door open slightly and peered through the resulting gap. Adam, Devin, Farrah, and Dahlia sat hunched over a small table in a muted conference. All were weary, and Farrah's face was pale from exhaustion. They had spent the day planning and investigating, but all for nought.

Frayne pushed the door open further and entered the room to stunned silence. Before he could speak, Farrah broke the stillness by leaping from her chair and flinging herself at him with such force that he staggered backwards and almost fell. A few tears of relief slipped unchecked from her eyes. The others soon followed. Devin laughed and slapped Frayne's back, Dahlia smiled and kissed his cheek, and Adam, the worry draining from his face, grasped Frayne's shoulder and did not let go. Farrah stepped back, and Adam grasped Frayne in a brief embrace. "Mate, I think it's time we took a break," he whispered.

Frayne and Farrah sat on the floor beside Dahlia's fire, watching as the embers slowly died. The men had resolved to spend the night on pallets on the floor, leaving the beds free for the women, but Farrah preferred to remain by Frayne. In the hours since he had returned, she had not left his side, her pale face and reddened eyes testaments to the anguish she had suffered during his absence. Now she leaned upon his shoulder, sleep gently drifting over her.

"Farrah?"

She turned her head slightly towards him in response.

"Farrah, will you marry me?"

She sat up, the tiredness quickly falling away to be replaced by delighted surprise. "Marry you?"

Frayne nodded, smiling in relief at the joy on her face, "I can't imagine my life without you, Farrah. I love you, and I want to be with you forever."

Farrah considered him carefully, but her smile did not falter, "I do not think that we can count on forever, Frayne. We're far too prone to accident and arrest."

"For the rest of our lives then, and we'll leave forever up to God."

She laughed, "I will marry you. And I'll love you for as long as I live. I have always loved you, you know. Right from the first moment I saw you, and you told me my mother must be blind to think me beautiful."

Frayne coloured, "What a little beast I was. If it helps, I did not believe the words even as I spoke them."

Farrah laughed again, "You can spend the rest of your life making it up to me, my darling Frayne.

He grinned, "Then I shall begin right now." He rose and moved towards the door, "Wait here a moment, please?"

Frayne slipped out of the room, leaving Farrah alone in a happy stupor. She could not remember the last time she had felt such joy. Her heart was full of it. Frayne returned a few minutes later, holding something small in both hands. He knelt beside her, took her hand, then hesitated. He gently placed a small ring in her palm, "I saved this for you." The look he gave her was an anxious one.

She studied the ring, a thin band of silver clasping a blue

stone. It was beautiful and familiar, though she did not know how, and something deep within her began to ache at the sight of it. She slipped it onto her finger, and then she knew. It was not her hand she saw before her, but her mother's. The same ring had graced that beloved hand and was such a part of it that Farrah could not imagine one apart from the other.

She moved her hand slowly, only now seeing how like her mother's it had become. How often had she watched Mrs Alves' hands kneading bread, cleaning dishes, holding tightly to her own? The ache grew within Farrah but could not dispel the joy that filled her. Tears of happiness and sorrow mingled together.

"I hope you don't mind," Frayne said hesitantly, "I know I should have given it to you before now. It should have always been yours, but recently, I hoped that when I did give it to you, it would mean more, as it does now."

Farrah laughed, though tears still filled her eyes, "I don't mind, I understand, but how did you find it?"

Frayne still looked uncertain, "I took it from her hand before they took her away. It was precious to her, so it was precious to me. It was the last thing I had of her, so I kept it, though now I can see how selfish it was. It always belonged to you."

Farrah smiled and shook her head, "No, I am glad you kept it as long as you did. My father gave it to our mother the day he asked her to marry him. He made it himself, with silver he bought and a precious stone he found during his travels." she wiped her eyes, then flung herself into his arms. "It is the most perfect gift that you could give me. Thank you, my beloved Frayne." She kissed him again and again, and they spent the rest of the night in laughter and conversation, speaking sweet words of little import that would linger in their minds for the rest of their lives.

CHAPTER NINETEEN

A new chapter began in their lives. Frayne and Farrah were married the following week in a small chapel twelve miles outside the city. They invited Bessie, the innkeeper's daughter, to join the ceremony as a bridesmaid. The young girl accepted their invitation graciously enough. However, in the days leading up to the wedding, she prepared for her office with all the injured dignity of a scorned lover—she truly had been infatuated with Frayne. Fortunately, her manner was greatly improved when Farrah suggested that they embellish the girl's dress with a pink silk sash, four lace flounces, and hidden pockets which could contain any number of sweets. Devin was quite taken with the child, and it was a joy to witness the transformation in his formidable face as he applauded Bessie's dress and helped her to stuff as many treats as possible into her pockets.

Besides Bessie and the priest, no one outside of the five witnessed the wedding. Devin gave Farrah away, and I am sure that images of his daughter, taken from him so long ago, danced through his mind as he placed her hand in Frayne's. Adam and Dahlia stood watch on either side of the couple as they pronounced their vows, and I am certain that no happier guardians have graced a wedding before or since.

When the ceremony was over, the five temporarily parted ways. Frayne and Farrah travelled north for several days until they reached a large house tucked quietly away in a valley beside a lake. It was a lovely thing and Frayne's wedding gift to Farrah. The day they arrived, the wind was still, and the lake transformed into glass. From a distance, the house, so close to the banks, appeared to be resting on the edge of a fallen silk of sky. As they grew closer, the reflection of the house materialised in the lake, and it looked as though two similar worlds had drawn together and, for a fleeting moment, were separated only by a thin blade of green.

It was an enchanted place, edged with orchards and guarded by forests—cut off from the world and adorned with the most beautiful memories. It was a home of laughter and happy secrets. At its centre, it held a promise—that one day, when the excitement of their lives in the city had faded, Frayne and Farrah would return here together, to walk hand in hand through the orchards once more, and sit, arms entwined, upon the wall of their secret garden, smiling as the last rays of the setting sun faded from their sight.

Devin and Dahlia returned together to the city, Dahlia to tend her shop and Devin to his rooms at the inn. Adam went his own way, with promises to follow Dahlia in a few weeks. Dahlia and Devin often sought each other's company during that time, as they had no other companions within the city. It was a welcome reminder of the lively days so recently passed. Most evenings, Dahlia joined Devin in the inn's taproom, partly for his company and partly because she feared what he may do if left to himself for too long. Devin's time with them had tempered him greatly, but anger and violence are not easily let go of, and Dahlia feared that if left alone, he would once again become driven by the crimson darkness that rested within him.

Perhaps it was well that the two of them had that time together. Although Frayne, Farrah, and Adam were all haunted by the demons of their past, Dahlia and Devin struggled with theirs the most. In each other, they found a confidant uniquely suited to understand their heartache, and they found family. To Devin, Dahlia was like a daughter. To Dahlia, Devin was, if not a father, then the closest she could ever come to accepting someone in that role.

One evening, Dahlia met Devin outside her shop, and they walked together towards the inn. The fading sun stole the warmth of the day, leaving a bitter chill hanging in the air. Dahlia gazed, unseeing, at her feet as she walked—she had slept poorly the night before, and whispers of her dreams haunted her still. She cast about her mind for anything to distract from the lingering shadows. She hesitated for a moment before saying, "Devin, may I ask, what was your daughter's name?"

Devin had been walking with his arms folded tightly against him for warmth, a distant expression upon his face. Her question dispelled the vacancy, and within his eyes, ire and agony danced together with the joy of memory.

"Anna, 'er name was Anna".

A small smile crept across Dahlia's mouth, "It is a sweet name."

Devin nodded in response, torment sketched across his face, but did not speak again.

Dahlia studied his creased visage. It seemed to her as though he was either born to wear pain or the anguish of the past had carefully shaped his features until they fitted the emotion perfectly. Some countenances seem designed for a particular emotion. She considered Adam's face, ever forefront in her mind. His face was sculpted for cheer—any other expression seemed foreign and ill-fitting—but pain suited Devin best.

He exhaled sharply, startling Dahlia, "My Cymbeline used to say Anna was the breath before laughter." The corners of his lips turned slightly upward, and he shook his head, "She was an angel."

Sorrow had entered Dahlia's eyes, "I once had a sister. I told her each day that she was my darling angel. She was beautiful and so different from me. She was sweetness and light." She passed a hand swiftly over her eyes, "She is a true angel now, or so I wish to believe. She left me for heaven after only five years."

Devin rubbed his breast as though the anguish within was a physical pain to be eased with a touch, "Some people are too good for this world."

Dahlia gently slipped her arm through his, "What hope does that leave the rest of us then?"

Devin rubbed his nose, "Don't know. The 'ope that we'll follow them someday I suppose."

Dahlia nodded despondently, and they hurried into the warmth of the lighted taproom.

Adam returned to the city three weeks later and went immediately to Dahlia's shop. Upon entering, he found her and Devin behind the counter, hunched over with laughter. Dahlia straightened with a cry and ran to the door when she saw Adam. He lifted her above his head and swung her about the room, but though his mouth smiled his delight, his eyes held no joy.

Gently, he set Dahlia down and turned to face Devin, his expression turning to one of shock. Swirls of purples and yellowing greens reached up from Devin's cheekbone to twine around his eye.

"What happened to you?"

Devin grimaced, but Dahlia spoke before he could open his mouth, "There were some unpleasantly drunk men at the inn one evening who made some impolite remarks towards me." she grinned, "Devin rendered them unconscious."

Adam raised an eyebrow in surprise, "How many men?"

Devin shrugged, "Four."

Now Adam's painted smile fell away, and his eyes laughed.

"And you, Adam, where did you hide?" Dahlia asked, taking his arm.

The laughter vanished as quickly as it had come, "Home, I went home."

Frayne and Farrah stood, hand in hand, before a peeling door. The building before them was flanked by handsome houses and seemed ill at ease, slouching between its dignified neighbours. Contrary to the peeling doorway and overgrown garden, the interior was not in terrible disrepair, but it exuded an air of fatigued dissatisfaction and had plainly stood empty for many years.

This lamentable building had once been home to Frayne and Farrah. For months, Frayne had worked to discover what had become of Mrs Alves' belongings. After much searching, he had located a copy of her will stating that all her earthly possessions were to fall to her daughter and son. Included among these possessions was the house. Tentatively, Farrah approached the doorway and paused, breath held, her fingers upon the handle. Frayne smiled at her reassuringly, and together they entered.

It was an odd feeling to walk through this building they had once known so well. It had become a shadow of its former self, a body with no spirit to illuminate it. Their memories hung thickly at the forefront of their minds, layering their vision. Farrah entered the kitchen, and for a moment, she could see her mother bending over the oven, then turning with a laugh to the place where a table had once stood—the place where a small girl had sat, sweet and painfully innocent, dipping her fingers into a mixing bowl. She closed her eyes to obscure the memory, then turned quickly from the room in search of Frayne.

Farrah found him in a small upstairs room, his eyes heavy with unshed tears. In his memory, he saw Mrs Alves, illuminated by soft candlelight, and heard a voice whispering, "My sweet…my dearly loved son…I shall not let you go, my Frayne."

"Frayne," Farrah's voice startled him back into the present, "let us leave."

He shook his head and gently took her arm, "One more room, Farrah."

Arms entwined, they climbed higher until they reached the room at the top of their house where they had once sat during the darkest period of their lives, two children knitted together by grief. That room alone was unchanged. Throughout the years, it had remained a place of limbo—a place of aching, anguish, and bleeding hearts. Mrs Alves had been the light and spirit of the home, and it had died with her, but this room lived on, sustained by grief, awaiting the time it would be needed again.

Now, Frayne and Farrah sat there once more, locked together in an embrace—two lovers sharing their present joys and past heartache. Their tears mingled together, washing over their wounds and gently closing the holes that had been opened in their hearts long ago by Death's cruel fingers. Some of the darkness that had plagued them for so long was overcome, and Farrah smiled, "Let's go home."

CHAPTER TWENTY

Seven months had passed since the wedding—seven months since Adam had last seen Frayne. Although Adam could not begrudge the couple their happiness in marriage, he had felt some degree of melancholy as he watched Frayne and Farrah leave the church. Frayne was and would always remain his friend, but Adam knew that marriage changes all other relationships. There were moments still when he missed the surety of their childhood—the days when he knew without a doubt that it would be just Frayne and Adam, pickpockets extraordinaire, the scourge of the gentry and all who opposed them—brothers, inseparable, forever.

That was Adam's dream. It was the guiding force within him, the desire for family, for intimacy. Beneath his beautiful words and easy humour, his heart was crossed with scars. He had been broken, cast out, betrayed, and forsaken, but he had also known love and acceptance, friendship, and joy, and it was to those things he cleaved. He loved Frayne with the steadfast devotion of a brother, but he knew that Frayne's loyalty now belonged elsewhere.

When the sun finally set upon their lives, it was Farrah who would be standing beside Frayne, and it was her name that would be remembered with his.

But Adam would not be left alone as he had once imagined. Now, there was Dahlia—sweet, gentle, and beautifully good waiting by his side. Adam had never considered marriage before, but as he spent more time in her company, the idea began to creep gently into his subconscious. He found her one evening, asleep in a chair by her fire, a small book sliding from her lap. He retrieved it lest the sound of it falling should wake her. Carefully, he reached forward to brush some unruly strands of hair from her face, and words heard long ago slipped to the forefront of his mind. "'One half of me is yours, the other half yours. Mine own, I would say; but if mine, then yours, and so all yours.'" he smiled slowly and whispered, "Until the end of time."

The newlyweds were greeted with much enthusiasm when they returned to the city. Dahlia immediately whisked Farrah away to her shop, leaving the others to make their own way. Devin's face was etched with a grin as he grasped Frayne's hand in greeting. Adam seemed pleased, though hesitantly so, and it quickly became evident to Frayne that a change had been wrought in his friend during his absence. Beneath Adam's ready smile, an unfamiliar apprehension darkened his eyes.

Night found Adam and Frayne together in an emptying taproom—Adam nursing a mug of dark, foul-smelling liquid and Frayne with a rapidly emptying bowl of stew to employ his hands. The other three had long since retired to their own rooms in various inns about the city. The day had been full of laughter and cheerful reminiscing, but now all pretence of pleasure had melted away, and apprehension stood stark upon Adam's face. He shifted his weight, his gaze wandering over each person in the room before raking across the table to his hands.

"After you left, I returned home."

Confusion and surprise chased each other across Frayne's face, "Home…to the quayside? Why?"

Adam shrugged, "Curiosity. Not much has changed—same houses, same quayside, same pervading stench. Same pub with its resident drunks."

A weight seemed to settle on Frayne's shoulders, "Did you see her?" The words crept from his mouth against his will.

Adam paused, contemplating his response, but for once his florid words failed him. "No. She's dead, Mate."

A numbing chill stole over Frayne, creeping through his body to his heart and blanketing his mind. "She is dead," he told himself, "Trudy is dead." but regardless of how many times he repeated that statement, the words did not touch him.

Unnerved by his own numbness, Frayne searched deep within his mind for the locked door that restrained his most abominable memories of the woman who had birthed him. She had given him life, but as if to devastate the wonder of that gift, she had brought him anguish, pain, and a desperate, unfulfilled longing. She had taught him to fear and shown him the face of hatred. Pain, fear, and hate—those were Trudy's only gifts, or so Frayne told himself. Every terror Frayne had faced since the day of his birth carried some trace of her, and hers was the face that lurked in the darkest shadows of his mind. She was the horror within him, and now she was gone. Where, then, was the relief, the elation?

Frayne flung wide the door within his mind. With

almost pleading desperation, he begged something to come. Something, anything to make him feel. The memories arrived slowly at first, mere impressions dancing through his mind, spinning across his senses—the smell of alcohol, the creak of loose floorboards, the sound of breaking glass. Then softly, a deep, almost forgotten aching emerged and gently wrapped itself about the numbness cocooning Frayne's heart. Satisfied, he pulled away and raised dry eyes to meet Adam's. He opened his mouth, composed, then flinched as though he had been struck. Memory after memory tore to the forefront of his mind, each carrying a pain made unbearable by suppression. Something deep within him had been unfettered, and his body shook with the force of it. Trudy's face appeared before him, and her voice echoed within his ears. His earliest memory was a shout, "Come here, you worthless lout!" and pain at the side of his head.

All was chaos within Frayne's mind as the past rived through him. Trudy loomed above him, each blow, insult, and scathing glance scoring his heart once more. The full weight of his mother's hatred towards him painted his heart, and this time, the brushstrokes were black.

Adam sat frozen with concern as he watched his friend shake. Finally, Frayne's mouth opened once more, "Why?" he gasped.

Adam understood. Why all this grief, why all this sorrow for a woman that he had loathed? "She was your mother. No amount of anger can change that. No matter how much you may wish it were not so, a part of you loved her."

"She was not my mother!" Frayne's shout echoed through the now-empty taproom. He sighed, weariness stealing across his face, "Do you see her in me, Adam?" His voice was gentle now, "Sometimes I do, just hints of her in the things I say, in my temper, my actions. In those moments, I revile myself more than I ever did her."

Adam shook his head, a bright film of tears colouring his eyes, "No, Mate, never."

Frayne nodded absentmindedly and lapsed into silence. The emotions that had surged within him just moments ago were fading as quickly as they had come, leaving his heart scarred and heavy with overwhelming exhaustion. Slowly, timidly, one last memory crept from behind the door in his mind. Frayne sat upon Trudy's lap—small and frail—her arms wrapped gently about him, rocking him to sleep. She leaned forward, her hair brushing his cheek, and whispered, "I love you, my son." In the memory, he blinked back the cloud of sleep and tears that obscured his vision, but it was Mrs Alves' face, not Trudy's, that gazed tenderly into his own. Frayne sighed and looked back at Adam, "Perhaps I will have a drink after all."

That night, Frayne fell asleep with Farrah's arms wrapped tightly about him, her fingers still damp with his tears. He dreamt of Trudy—she stood in the kitchen of their house, looking down at the uneven wooden floorboards—they had not lain flat since the day that Frayne had pried them up to hide a small, golden treasure. Lost in contemplation, Trudy did not seem to see her son, though he stood only an arm's length away from her. He was taller than her now—much taller—and looking down upon her, Frayne noticed for the first time how truly small she was. Not only was she small in height, but the rage that had once given her stature now seemed weak, overshadowed by a sense of insecurity that surrounded her.

Trudy had always been afraid, Frayne realised—afraid, desperate, and hurt. Her anger was her shield, but foolishly, she had wielded it against the only person in her world who was capable of loving her. She was a pitiable figure and seeing her as such eased some of the pain and fear within Frayne. He knew that she would no longer haunt him, but he could not forgive her, not then, perhaps he never would—she had coloured his body black, purple, and a vivid red, and his heart likewise. That broken part of him would always belong to her, but it would grow smaller with each passing year, and perhaps in time, it would disappear altogether.

CHAPTER TWENTY-ONE

Mr Simmons, my story now hastens to its end. I find myself clutching at it, pulling it out, as if, by delaying, I may change its conclusion. For all that this story details a life, it is beautifully brief, as Frayne would have wished it to be.

A change had arrived, slowly, subtly, but welcomed by many. A growing population inevitably precedes an increase in lawlessness, and those in power finally awoke from their great indifference to discover the world rife with crime. The danger that had once stayed hidden in dim, twisted streets had spilt over into the light. Criminal gangs had grown in number and influence, but it was in the men who stepped forward to oppose them that the greater darkness lay.

I have always harboured a particular disdain for thief-takers. Many were convicted criminals who had betrayed those they worked with to save their own lives. Once acquitted, they acted as a form of law enforcement, albeit for a gratuity. As noble and respectable as this profession appeared, many merely used it as a front. Their previous connections in the criminal underworld gave these men the unique opportunity to establish a new vein of illegal activities that took advantage of criminals and innocents alike. They sent droves of men to the gallows—some guilty, some virtuous, and some induced into committing felonies by the thief-takers themselves. These men grew unchecked in power and wealth, spreading the stain of corruption throughout the city. Thievery was no longer a game but a violent, dangerous pursuit.

Something had changed within Frayne as well. His childish delight and eager restlessness, once an easy part of him, no longer came naturally. The joyfulness that had once resided within him had slipped, though he clutched it about him still, like an ageing man clinging desperately to the remnants of his youth. Outwardly, he seemed content, unaltered, but beneath that visage lay a new shadow. It was as though Frayne knew, deep within his being, that something in his life had ended. Unavoidable darkness lay on his horizon, and he was ambling towards it with the weary acceptance that all must shoulder in the end.

He knew, I think, that his days of crime were at an end. In this new environment, it was too dangerous, and with his face known to lawmakers within the city, it would have been the height of folly to draw attention to himself. Frayne could have left the city, they all could have—it would have been easy enough to move, to disappear into a new city and resume their illicit affairs, but something held him there. Perhaps it is human nature to find comfort in a familiar environment and remain despite the dangers and limitations that such a place may present. It's possible that Frayne expected things to change and that he held onto the hope that life could return to what it had once been. If so, then it was hope that was his undoing, foolish, misguided hope.

It was a thief-taker who caught him. It seems somewhat

ironic to me that this particular arrest came months after Frayne had ceased his illegal activities, but such is the way of life. He was having lunch at a small pub when the men came for him. At first, there was only one, staggering, then dropping into a chair before Frayne, loud, enthusiastic, and seemingly inebriated out of his senses.

"I know you!" the man nodded vigorously, "I do, I know you. You're one of those, those," he waved a hand as if hoping to lay ahold of his next words, "highway fellows!" he finished triumphantly. Frayne calmly stood, but the man grabbed his wrist and, with surprising force, pulled Frayne across the table towards him, "I know you," he hissed, and there was no smell of alcohol upon his breath, "I know you, and this time, your luck has run out." Two men now appeared behind Frayne and, grasping his shoulders, forced him back into his seat. "You have led us on a merry dance," the man across from Frayne leaned forward conspiratorially, "but now it's time to take your bow." Two circles of iron were clapped about Frayne's wrists, and, unresisting, he was led away.

Past experience had taught the men to be wary of Frayne. He was taken from the pub and transported rapidly to the prison in a covered cart. There, he was confined almost immediately within a strong room, placed in a wooden chair, then left, hands still manacled, with a jailer. The man clearly doubted those measures would be enough to prevent Frayne from escaping again. No one had ever left the strongroom of his own accord, but to the jail keeper, who was a devoutly religious man, the stout wooden door and iron bars seemed paltry compared to Frayne's reported otherworldly abilities. To be certain of his prisoner's security, he attached heavy irons to each of Frayne's legs, then secured them to the floor with a horse padlock for extra measure. He looked into his prisoner's eyes for a moment and saw—I know not what—perhaps some rekindled fire, fury, or a shred of madness, for he took one stumbling step backwards. Hesitantly, he drew forth a thin chain from under his shirt, on which was threaded a small iron cross. He unclasped it from his throat and, with a slight tremble to his hands, fastened it about Frayne's neck. He stepped back to survey his work, then, without a word, turned and practically fled the cell.

For the next three days, Frayne attempted to resign himself to his situation. Something had changed deep within him, and he saw his imprisonment as an inevitable step on the slow, humiliating journey that he knew to be his last. And it was humiliating—his notoriety drew curious visitors to the prison. The guards, ever the shrewd businessmen, capitalised on the opportunity, charging each visitor two shillings to peer through a small viewing window at the disgraced highwayman.

Men and women from every level of society came to see him—some laughed, some gasped, some merely stared. The turnkey swiftly lost his fear of his prisoner and took back the cross he had bestowed upon him. I am sure that it is difficult to fear a man who is caged like an animal and broken in spirit. However, baited animals fight the fiercest, and the same is true of men—a fact that the jailkeeper seemed unaware of, for he began to find pleasure in insulting and tormenting Frayne. He never took it too far, for he was a restrained man—a quality much desired in jailers—but he found immense satisfaction in offering the frequent barbed comment and spilling Frayne's water as he carried it to him, so there was never quite enough to drink.

Outwardly, Frayne bore these petty insults with immense grace, recognising them as paltry attempts at assertion, but within himself, another voice whispered, rousing him to ire. Each insult from his jailer and each pitying glance from his frequent visitors lodged like a barb within him. Slowly, the weight of indifference slipped from his shoulders, and a fierce determination began to burn again in his heart. For that, I owe his keeper a great thanks.

It pains me to admit that it was not until the third day after his arrest that Frayne's friends discovered what had befallen him. Farrah was not immediately concerned when she noticed her husband's absence, as it was not uncommon for Frayne to vanish with Adam for hours, if not days, without prior warning. However, by the second day, his continued non-appearance became unnerving.

Since the five had abandoned thievery, they no longer gathered together each day as they had once done. Therefore, it took another day for Farrah to get word to them all. Adam had been the main problem, as he had left the city without warning to watch a play in a town further north. At Farrah's bidding, he returned hastily to the city and arrived at Dahlia's shop a week and a half after Frayne's arrest.

"What has happened? Where is Frayne?" Adam burst in without preamble.

Dahlia turned to smile at him as he entered, but the rest remained stony-faced.

"'E was arrested nearly two weeks ago now." Devin answered, "'E's kept in a strong room, chained to the ground."

"Two weeks?" Adam dropped into a chair. "Two weeks with no word or hint of escape?"

Devin nodded, "I went to see 'im. They're charging two bleeding shillings to take a look at 'im, like 'e's some sort of curiosity. I thought I could slip 'im some instruments or 'elp 'im escape, but the guards watched too carefully. 'E didn't even look up at me, just stared at the ground, loaded down with irons, pale as the moon."

Adam glanced towards Farrah, whose complexion had turned as chalky as her husband's. Gently, he laid his hand upon hers, "'Give sorrow words.'" he murmured, "'The grief that does not speak whispers the o'er-fraught heart, and bids it break.'"

She nodded, and quiet tears slipped from her eyes.

Dahlia placed her arm about her friend's shoulders, "Farrah," she whispered, "Frayne has not been bested yet. He shall escape."

Farrah nodded slightly in response.

"I shall go to the prison." Adam announced, standing, "I will find some means of aiding Frayne."

Concern flashed across Dahlia's face, "No, Adam, the guards know you. It would be the height of folly."

Adam smiled slightly, "Frayne is my brother, and I owe him my life. To turn away now because I fear paying that debt would mark me a coward."

"So, you would be a hero and die in his place?" Dahlia demanded.

"'Cowards die many times before their deaths; the valiant never taste death but once.'"

"There is no valiance in hanging."

"I love Frayne, Dahlia. I love him as my brother and as my dearest friend, and I shall not see him die."

"But Frayne would not care to see you die in his place, Adam." Farrah gently interjected, "Do not lose your wits in a foolish fit of melodrama. Do not break my sister's heart." She laid her hand upon Dahlia's, "Do not break our hearts because you did not pause to consider. If you go to the prison, go in disguise. Take nothing with you and speak to no one, especially Frayne. We shall help him as we can, but we shall not have you die with him."

Adam nodded, knowing how much it cost her to speak so. "I am sorry, Dahlia, for vexing you so." He said and bent to kiss her.

Dahlia pulled backwards that she might better see his face, "'I would not wish any companion in the world but you.'" She whispered.

Adam smiled slightly, "Nor I, but you. I shall keep my head and my neck too and return within a couple of hours." he looked to Devin, who had remained silent throughout the exchange, "Will you remain here in case of trouble?"

The big man nodded, then lapsed back into thought, his eyes full of misgivings.

CHAPTER TWENTY-TWO

It had been a week since Frayne's arrest, and his incarceration was wearing furiously at his patience. As his indifference to his fate faded, he started contemplating various methods of escape, but success eluded him. On the morning of the fourth day, he had had the good fortune to discover a small nail on the floor within his reach. With some practice, he found that he could open the horse padlock that held his leg irons to the floor and free himself to move about his cell. Although this accomplishment later won Frayne much praise from the general populace, I assure, you Mr Simmons that such a trick is well within the abilities of any man with some knowledge of locks. Indeed, any common smith could replicate Frayne's efforts with ease.

Frayne relished the minor independence that the chains had denied him. He spent the entire day inspecting each centimetre of his room for a means of escape. There was his chair, but it was an old spindly thing, and certainly no match for the strength of the stone walls and ceiling. There was a cot, which he had been unable to reach while his legs remained shackled, that he now took the opportunity to lay on whenever he tired of exploring his cell. The sheets upon the cot were thin and not long enough to form a rope that would reach from his cell to the ground. Escape from his tiny window was further prevented by iron bars, which, despite his best efforts, remained immovable. Finally, and most interestingly, there was a chimney, but when Frayne attempted to crawl up it, he found his way blocked by a long iron bar. Escape seemed impossible, so he fixed his leg irons to the floor in time for his evening inspection, then freed himself again afterwards and promptly fell asleep upon the cot.

This small freedom was curtailed the next day when Frayne's keepers made a surprise visit to his cell and caught him wandering about the room, free of his chains. The turnkey stood in the open door, mouth agape, fear once more creeping into his eyes. Frayne offered him a lazy grin and wondered whether he should rush the man and attempt to break past him and out of the cell. These thoughts came to a sudden halt as four men ran in at the jailer's call and thrust Frayne back into his chair with enough force to run a crack through its leg. They reattached his chains to the floor and secured the padlock. The small nail went unnoticed but was kicked accidentally by one of the men into a corner beyond Frayne's reach.

The jailer stood before Frayne, sweating and contemplating his restraints. I believe that the man would have happily draped Frayne's entire body in irons and pinned him to the floor for the fear of God and the Devil had been stamped back into him. Instead, he contented himself with ordering a heavy pair of handcuffs for Frayne and checking the security of the horse padlock twice before leaving him alone.

Frayne remained in his cell for the next week. The

handcuffs posed no inconvenience to him, as he quickly discovered he could remove them with ease. Adam had first demonstrated this art to Frayne one cold, wet day when their home was still high amongst the city's rooftops.

There were few passersby that week due to the weather, so Adam took it upon himself to fill the day with lessons that he insisted were necessary for Frayne's survival.

"Watchmen," he began, holding high a pair of handcuffs, "use these."

Frayne stared intently at the metal bands that swung before his face. Adam seemed to be expecting a reply of some sort, but the words he wished to hear eluded Frayne.

"You stole them?" he asked.

Adam rolled his eyes in an exaggerated display of exasperation. "Found them. Right, say you get caught."

"Why should I get caught?" A note of belligerence crept into Frayne's voice.

"'Cause you're still a prince playing at being a beggar." Frayne glared at him, and Adam rolled his eyes again. "Fine, say I get caught. There's a lovely lady so enhanced by my pretty words…"

"Entranced."

Adam paused, "What?"

"Entranced by your pretty words."

"Right, moved to tears by my plight, she don't notice me taking her purse." He grinned and winked conspiratorially at Frayne, "But a big ugly watchman sees. He drags me away," Frayne laughed as Adam staggered across the cobbled street, fighting an imagined man, "and chains me to this rail." Adam paused to fasten one wrist in the cuffs, loop the chain around an iron rail, and fasten the other wrist. "There, I'm chained. What now?"

Frayne smiled slightly, "You escape?"

"Yes!" Adam nodded triumphantly at his friend, "I

escape." He gazed after the imaginary watchman and shouted, "Come back you sod! I'm a man under this dirt, not an animal! 'If you prick us do we not bleed? If you tickle us do we not laugh? If you poison us do we not die? And if you wrong us shall we not revenge?' By God, I shall have my revenge! And then," he bent his head to the cuffs, "I can just..." He swore. "Should come straight off..."

Frayne began to laugh as Adam wrestled ineffectively with the cuffs. After a few minutes, he held up one hand triumphantly, the wrist badly chafed but free from the cuffs.

"There!"

"And what if the watchman decides to use a rope instead?" Frayne asked.

Adam scowled, "Then you'd better pray you have a knife with you. Here, your turn." Frayne glanced dubiously at Adam. "'S not hard. They're all the same size, and we've got small hands. Just use your teeth to slip them off. Here," he clapped the handcuffs about Frayne's wrists, smiling apologetically, "'I must be cruel, only to be kind.'"

Alone in his cell, Frayne practised slipping the handcuffs on and off. It was reassuring that he could remove them at his pleasure, but without a means of unlocking the horse padlock and freeing his legs, his chances of escape seemed slim. He had been monitored closely since his jailor found him walking about his cell. Initially, he had attempted to move his captors, if not to pity, then at least into a sense of security by chafing his wrists raw against the manacles and slumping weakly upon the floor whenever he was visited. He had made some attempts at pleading, and though it wore at his pride, it seemed to have the desired effect of moving at least one man to compassion and convincing the rest that their charge was well and truly secure.

The day after Adam returned to the city, Frayne awoke to shouts and the sound of footsteps clattering past his cell door. He was sure he had not slept long but could not guess the time. He paused to think. He had already been visited three times by his keepers, so they would not disturb him again until morning, and though faint light still thrust itself through the bars of his window, the night could not be far behind.

Frayne turned his musings to the clamour that had woken him. Once, such a flurry of activity would have sparked excitement and hope within him, but his mind felt muffled in heavy exhaustion. He called for the guards that normally stood watch outside of his door but received no response. His lethargy fell away then—he pulled his handcuffs off, wincing as they dragged over his raw skin, then began furiously twisting at one of the links that chained his leg irons to the floor. He had no plan in mind but trusted his instincts to carry him through until a plan had formed.

Frayne was rather surprised when the link snapped, but without hesitation, he pulled the chain away, tucked the broken link into a pocket in his shirt, and stood, free of all restraints but his leg irons. He wore one on each ankle and the two cuffs were joined by a chain. Frayne contemplated breaking those too, but the chain was thick, so he settled for pulling the cuffs up to his calves and securing them there with strips of cloth torn from his shirt. He paused then, considering. The window was highly fortified and the door impassable, making the brick chimney the most likely means of escape if he could remove the iron bar. He picked up his wooden chair and hurled it against the wall, wincing as it splintered loudly and then clattered to the floor. He gathered the pieces and used them to chip away at the mortar that held the bricks together, finally pulling enough away to loosen the bricks and make a wide hole in the chimney. Using the broken link he had tucked in his pocket, he wrenched the iron bar from the chimney and, taking the bar with him, climbed to the room above.

Frayne emerged into a small room. It had once held rebels, and was appropriately fortified, but it was a long time since it had been occupied. His eyes wandered around the sparse space with curiosity and came to light upon a large nail, which he quickly gathered into his pocket. Coming to the door, he removed the nut from the lock and smiled slightly as the door swung open before him. He was beginning to enjoy this endeavour.

When Frayne reached the next door, his good mood quickly faded. The door was fastened on the far side by a metal bolt, so he faced an impenetrable expanse of thick wood. He attempted to pry the boards apart with the metal rod he had extracted from the chimney but was unsuccessful. He eventually resigned himself to hammering away at the wall next to the door, though each loud blow only heightened his fear of discovery. After much effort, he broke through to the room beyond and reached his arm through the gap to dislodge the bolt on the other side.

Frayne cautiously entered the next room and found himself in the prison chapel. A tall pulpit dominated the small room, facing towards a simple altar. Wooden benches tucked behind a wall of spiked iron bars acted as pews for the prisoners. The whole room exuded an air of cold discipline, the bare stone walls and floor adding to the overwhelming sense of dejection that pervaded every corner of the prison. Frayne climbed to the top of the spikes and broke one off to add to his growing collection of tools.

Frayne paused before the chapel door and surveyed the room once more. He tried to think of the last time he had been in a church. Religion had long seemed to be a comfortable, natural thing to him. He had never considered it while he had lived with Trudy, but he had always suspected Mrs Alves of having some affection towards God. When he had thought about it, he had always imagined the Lord of Heaven to be very much like his mother—gentle, compassionate, and with a special love for stray children.

Frayne grinned at a memory. The last time he had been in a church, he had stolen a loaf of bread from the altar. He and Adam had not eaten for a few days, and the great door was left unlocked. It had been an easy enough matter to enter unnoticed, and since he knew that Mrs Alves would not have minded a hungry child finding satiation in her stores of food, he was certain that God wouldn't either. With that in mind, he felt no guilt in taking the loaf of bread and the large cup of wine that stood beside it. He had returned the cup two days later, which Adam assured him would be enough to avoid divine retribution.

Frayne took one last sweeping glance around the room, then left the chapel easily enough through a door that opened on the inside. He was immediately faced by another stout door that stood between the chapel and what was sure to be the leads. This was framed in stone walls and held in place by strong metal hinges. A lock, guarded by a wooden box, prevented Frayne from moving any further. Night had well and truly fallen, and the pervading gloom that diminished Frayne's vision now seemed to seep into his spirits. His leg irons chafed against his calves, and the scabs on his wrists had cracked, sending thin lines of blood trickling down onto his blistered hands. The cold enveloped him, and sleep pressed heavily upon his eyelids, but with a great sense of effort, he shook it off and sought to prise away the box with the aid of the chapel spike and the large nail that he had discovered in the first room. Within twenty minutes, he had wrenched the box free, and triumphantly opened the lock and continued through the prison.

At this point, Frayne began to hope that he was almost through. He was unsure how long he had been away from his cell, but he knew he had travelled a considerable distance. He was still wary of discovery but was beginning to feel the elation that the sudden hope of freedom carries. After a time, he came to another door, but even that could not dampen his spirits, not now that he believed himself so close to the end. It was guarded by a box and by more bolts, bars, and locks than any door he had ever faced before. He began by attacking the box that covered the main lock but did not make any progress. Next, he attempted to force the wooden fillet of the door away from the main post using his metal rod as a lever. Much to Frayne's surprise, the whole board came free, taking the box with it, and rendering the door easily passable.

He continued on, passing through another door that opened smoothly from the inside and then working his way upward to the roof. He looked down from a great height to the lighted city streets below, breathed deeply of the cold night air, and laughed—softly, for he was still aware that his freedom was not yet absolute—but with great relief. Frayne surveyed the houses that bordered the prison, his eagerness to be far away from there increasing with each frustrating minute that passed. The closest roof was no less than eighteen metres below Frayne. To jump from that height would be to test death. To hang from the prison roof and then allow himself to fall would guarantee that his legs would break—neither option seemed particularly enticing.

He remembered the sheets back on the cot in his cell.

They were not long enough to reach from his high cell window to the ground, but surely, they could get him close enough to this roof to avoid disaster. It appeared to be the only option, though he was reluctant to return to the heart of the prison. His guards could be back at their posts soon, or if they had already returned, they could be scouring the prison for him. However, seeing no alternative, Frayne turned his back on the city lights and descended into the prison.

His return journey was significantly swifter as he had left each door he had first passed through open behind him. He ran quickly and softly and reached the rebel's cell within minutes. Frayne cautiously descended the chimney, and then paused to survey his cell. If the guards had returned, they had left no sign of their presence, as the room was exactly how he had left it. Perhaps then, they were still occupied by whatever disturbance had drawn them away in the first place. Still, Frayne had no intention of being caught due to folly, so he entered the room hunched over in a crawl, trusting the pervading darkness to mask his movements. He reached the bed without incident and stripped it of its coverings, then slowly made his way back to the chimney.

Once again, he found himself atop the prison, looking down upon the roof that could be his salvation. He tied a sheet and his blanket firmly together, then used the spike from the chapel to secure his makeshift rope to the outside wall of the prison. Frayne looked dubiously at his handiwork, unsure if it would take his weight, but as he had no other means to lessen his descent, he trusted himself to the rope and made it to the second roof without injury. Once there, he found the garret window open. He entered through it, then silently descended two flights of stairs that ended next to an open doorway. Gentle lamplight spilt out of the room beyond, and Frayne could hear the low murmur of voices. He moved slowly towards the door, hoping to walk silently past, but as he stepped forward, his leg irons made a clinking sound, and he heard a woman within cry, "Lord, what noise is that?"

Frayne rushed back to the garret where he rested for three hours until the household was in bed. At last, he descended the stairs again in a final bid for freedom. The room at the foot of the stairway was empty, and Frayne hurried past it, then down another set of steps to the entryway. As he approached the street door, he heard voices nearing the stairs behind him. Unwilling to hesitate any longer, Frayne rushed out the door, leaving it open behind him—rejoicing that he was a free man.

CHAPTER TWENTY-THREE

What happened next, Frayne was never able to completely recall. Heavy tiredness had settled about him as he rushed through the darkened streets, paying no heed to the direction he took but trusting in his feet to know the way. He remembered arriving at Dahlia's shop, holding Farrah tightly against him, her tears of relief seeping through his thin shirt, and laying down on an old mattress. There had been a question asked at some point, an important question, but it was quickly lost amidst the haze that shrouded his mind.

"Where is Adam?" were the first words Dahlia uttered upon beholding Frayne. He had looked at her uncomprehendingly and muttered something unintelligible that did nothing to ease her concern.

Farrah examined Frayne and discovered the wounds on his wrists and legs, then, touching his forehead, announced, "He has a fever."

"Then he could not have escaped alone, so where is Adam?" Dahlia persisted.

"I am sure that he is safe." Farrah rested her hand upon

Dahlia's arm, "We shall find him in the morning, but for now, Frayne must rest."

Devin placed his arm around Dahlia, "If Frayne's not talking by tomorrow, I'll come with you to the prison in case Adam's still there. Don't worry, 'e'll be fine."

The night that ensued felt like an eternity to Frayne. The fever ravished his weakened body and danced with his mind, dragging the night out in endless darkness. Voices called out to him, and strange visions wended their way before his eyes. Carriages seemed to hurtle through Frayne's room. Fires burned at his wrists and ankles, a man was screaming his name, and faintly, behind it all, he could hear the persistent creaking of a gallows.

The nightmares quieted, and now Frayne could make out a small figure that looked like an angel hovering above him, its wings brushing gently across his face. Its touch was cool and soothing against his feverish skin, and when it opened its mouth, it spoke in Farrah's voice, calling his name, whispering for him to come back to her.

Frayne felt himself sit up. In his hand, he held his watch. It was cold, hard, reassuring, and as familiar to him as his own face. Its hands read half an hour past 10 o'clock. It felt late, though faint daylight still surrounded him, and he could not recall where he was or how he had found his way there.

"Frayne?" A voice called.

Surprised, he looked up into the smiling face of Mrs Alves.

"Frayne, it is time for you to leave that here."

Gently, she took the watch from his hands and placed it beside him. As it left her hands, the slight tick that had marked its life came to a sudden and silent stop.

Frayne gazed intently up at his mother, "Is this death?"

She smiled again, but sadness tinged the edges, "It is a new beginning."

He shook his head slowly, resolutely, "It is too soon. I cannot leave Farrah."

"Death is not always gracious." The pain of memory swept over her face, "But she has the strength to face this," a hint of pride coloured her voice, "she is my daughter."

"I cannot leave her, not now, please. I promised her a lifetime together."

His mother's smile was tender, regretful, "Change demands sacrifice of us all." Slowly, she leaned forward and kissed his brow, "Find peace, my beloved Frayne."

Frayne's fever broke on the evening of the fourth day. Farrah had remained by his bedside throughout his sickness and was the first to see his eyes open. The bright gleam of delirium had vanished, leaving behind a determined intensity born from the knowledge that he had been given a second chance at life.

"Farrah?" He struggled to rise into a sitting position, but Farrah gently pushed him back down.

"Hush, Frayne, you have been unwell. You must rest now."

"No, Farrah, I wish to leave, right now, to leave the city."

His words came slowly and laboriously. Suddenly, his mind was filled with the memory of waking up in another bed, the same sombre face peering down at him and Farrah, with an imperious toss of her small head announcing, "I'm Farrah, it means beautiful".

Frayne laughed, though it caused him pain, and continued, "I want to return to our house by the lake, to have ten children and live there, happily, for the rest of our lives."

Farrah smiled, but before she could reply, Dahlia dashed into the room and dropped heavily into a chair next to Farrah.

"Thank goodness you are awake! It is Adam. He was arrested at the prison, aiding your escape, and now he is to be hanged."

Farrah took her friend's arm, "Dahlia, please, you must calm yourself. Fraye is still weak. Adam will not be hanged. We shall not allow it."

The smile dropped from Frayne's face, "I did not see Adam at the prison." Slowly the details of his flight returned to him, "Was he there the night that I escaped?"

Dahlia nodded, "He went to speak to you, to help you. We had heard nothing from you for weeks." A slightly accusatory tone laced her words, but Frayne did not appear to notice.

"Have you seen him yet, Dahlia?"

"No, Devin did not want me to take a risk until I had spoken with you, but he visited the guards."

"There was a disturbance the night I escaped. The guards were distracted, so I was able to get away."

Dahlia nodded again vigorously, "That was Adam. A man recognised him, so he ran away through the prison. Apparently causing havoc as he went." Her face grew sober, "They have accused him of killing one of the guards, but I know Adam, he would never hurt anyone."

For a moment, Frayne remembered Adam, young and desperate, standing over the body of a boy, a brick clutched tightly in his hand.

"Dahlia, desperation will move a man to strange feats."

She stared resolutely into Frayne's eyes, "Never."

Frayne turned uneasily back to Farrah, "I will disguise

myself and go to the prison, I cannot see them holding Adam for long lest he escapes, so we must act quickly."

"No." Farrah pushed her husband firmly back onto the bed, "Why are you men so foolishly impulsive? Adam decided upon the same approach, and now he is imprisoned. You are weak, and your mind is clouded. You must rest. Dahlia and Devin will visit Adam to assess his situation while you contrive a plan. Then, and only then, shall we take action. I know Adam is your brother, but he just sacrificed his freedom to return you yours. To risk capture now would be to belittle that sacrifice."

Dahlia nodded in reluctant agreement, and Frayne followed her example. He knew that what Farrah said was true. Exhaustion was quickly creeping back into his limbs and wrapping around his thoughts.

He smiled reassuringly and reached out to take Dahlia's hand, "Do not fear Dahlia. Adam is my dearest friend, and I owe him my life. I shall not allow any harm to come to him." Frayne allowed his heavy eyelids slide shut, and his last thought was of Adam.

CHAPTER TWENTY-FOUR

Dahlia shivered as she passed through the stone corridors of the prison, Devin at her side. She had not been there since the day that she and Farrah had worked to free the boy, Christopher. After that, Dahlia had hoped she would never have cause to step foot in that wretched place again. She pulled the hood of her cloak closer to her face as they neared the guards, but none were the same men that she had met previously. Even if they were, I am sure they would not have recognised the anxious, pale-faced, slip of a girl as the vibrant, lively woman who had visited them before.

A small handful of coins guaranteed them an audience with Adam in his cell. Though his hair was tousled, and his nose bloodied, his smile remained unchanged, firmly set in defiance of the grim sentence that hung over him. His wrists and ankles were cuffed and attached to a long chain that was stapled firmly to the floor.

Dahlia rushed forward to offer him an awkward embrace, "They searched us when we arrived, Adam." She whispered, "We could not risk bringing anything."

He nodded, "I know, it is alright. Did Frayne make it out?"

Devin stepped forward, "Thanks to you. 'E was ill for a time, but 'e's up now, 'e'll get you out of this."

Adam smiled slightly and shook his head, "'I have touched the highest point of all my greatness; and from that full meridian of my glory I haste now to my setting'."

Dahlia grasped his hand, "Adam, do not speak in such a way. Frayne will not allow you to die."

"'The game is up', Dahlia. If it is my time to meet Death, I shall shake his hand with my head held high and no regrets colouring my heart."

"No!" Anger and fear leant volume to her voice.

Devin looked anxiously towards the door, beyond which the guards waited, but they did not stir.

"No, Adam." Gently, she took his face in her shaking hands, "I have watched as all those I loved left this world before I could bear to let them go. You are most dear to my heart, the one I wish to spend the rest of my life with. I shall not have you taken from me now." She stared adamantly into his eyes, "Trust in me. I shall not fail you."

Adam smiled and kissed her forehead, leaving behind small flecks of blood that stood out like rubies against her pale skin, "I know that Frayne will free me. I have complete confidence in him." He turned and embraced Devin, concern showing through his smile for a brief moment. "Take care of her, please," he whispered, "she does not have the strength to endure this."

Devin nodded and grasped his arm, "I'll tend 'er like she was my own daughter." Tenderly, the large man placed his hands upon Dahlia's shoulders and gently led her out of the cell.

Adam watched them go. A grim resignation had settled

upon him the moment the irons had clapped about his wrists, but now, slivers of hope were piercing through. His jailer entered the cell, his head held high, and a look of immense satisfaction splashed across his features. He surveyed Adam's bindings, then touched the iron cross that hung about his neck as if in gratitude.

"You have two more days." he informed his prisoner, "Perhaps now is the time to pray that God will pardon your tainted soul, lest you be damned for all eternity."

The man's face was a mask of righteous concern, but his voice implied that eternal damnation was a far lighter punishment than Adam deserved.

Adam looked thoughtfully back at his keeper, and then his face split apart in an unholy smile. He laughed, though his eyes were as cold and merciless as the iron about his jailer's neck. "'I think the devil will not have me damned, lest the oil that's in me should set hell on fire'."

The man stumbled backwards a step, then turned and walked deliberately from the room,"Let the Devil save you then."

It is easy, looking backwards, to see the tangled web of history, emotions, and circumstances that resolved themselves into a single thread of decision. Hindsight can be a cruel gift. With that gift, and some degree of regret, I now look retrospectively at Dahlia.

I believe that more than anything, Dahlia wished to be like her departed sister—a creature of sweetness and light, loving and beloved, beautiful, innocent, an angel. That was the face she wore and the spirit she tried to carry within her, but beneath that, and beneath the patches on her heart and the numbness that engulfed her memory, was something darker, more feral, that no mask of angelic goodness could conceal forever. Deep within Dahlia was a wounded animal—driven by fear and love. The broken child that she had once been had not grown up. It was buried within her, and now it whispered fragments of its forgotten pain up into her mind—a desperate cry of impending loss. There are no greater motivators than love and fear. Combined, the two have the power to bring about indescribable pain. This is what retrospect has shown me, Mr Simmons, but the cruelty of it is that the understanding has come too late. At the time, all were blind and helpless to prevent the anguish that Dahlia would cause.

When Dahlia returned from the prison, she went to seek out Farrah. She found her friend alone in the stables outside the city, attending to one of the horses.

"Did you see Adam?" Farrah asked. "Is he well?"

Dahlia passed a hand over her reddening eyes, "He is alive, but not for much longer, I fear. He has given up, Farrah," her voice broke. "He has given up, and now he will be taken from me."

"No, Dahlia, do not give up hope, not yet. Frayne will not let him die. He will have a plan. You must trust in him." She reached out to take Dahlia's arm, but her friend pulled away from her touch.

"You do not understand Farrah."

Farrah's face darkened, "You are wrong. I understand more than anyone else could."

Dahlia shook her head, agitated now, "No, you do not see, you do not see because you love Frayne, but he is not God, Farrah. He is not all-powerful. Every man has his limit, and Frayne has reached his. I was foolishly blind to remain still, doing nothing. My faith was well-founded but misplaced. I see that now."

The concern on Farrah's face was deepening.

"Dahlia…"

Her friend's eyes were wild, "He will hang tomorrow, Farrah. I heard one of the guards say it. It is too late now."

"No." Farrah clutched at Dahlia's arms. "It is not too late, Dahlia. If I have to take apart the gallows with my own hands, I shall. We will not allow Adam to die."

Dahlia's face was raked with misery, "I told you once, Farrah, that neither Adam nor Frayne would grow to be old men. It is as true today as it was then, but though I always knew it, I now find myself unable to face it. I cannot stand back and let him die. If it is in my power to act, Farrah, I will do it, no matter the cost, or I will die with him."

Farrah wordlessly took her sister into her arms, as she had done many times before when they were girls. They stood together for a time, Dahlia shaking with inconsolable grief and Farrah clutching her tightly so that Dahlia would not see the hopeless tears that fell silently from her eyes.

That evening, the four sat together in Dahlia's living room, hope and despair mingling as they turned their attention towards Frayne. Mere days before, he had been cast adrift in a state of delirium, but now he sat tall and self-assured, colour and strength already returning to his frame.

"I know a way in which we can save Adam." He smiled reassuringly at Dahlia, "It will not be without risk, but I believe it will work. I have to believe it."

Dahlia shifted uncomfortably, but Frayne pressed on.

"Adam will be taken to the gallows on a wooden cart, with only his hands bound, which will give us ample opportunity to free him. I believe I can discern the route they will take, but I must leave now, if I am to have everything in place by morning. I have told Farrah all, so she will explain while I am gone." He rose, "I shall be back before dawn."

He bent to kiss Farrah but paused as a quiet tapping echoed from the shop door back into the apartment.

Dahlia raised her head wearily, "It is a customer. Some of my wealthier patrons prefer the cloak of darkness."

Frayne smiled gently at her, "I shall tell him to return next week as I leave."

Dahlia nodded gratefully, then watched with Farrah as Frayne slipped through the door into the empty shop and out into the night.

Frayne stared in astonishment at the men who waited before Dahlia's door. There were five, their swords and grim expressions of triumph as familiar as the cold iron handcuffs that their leader proffered to Frayne.

"It seems that, once again, your luck has run out." The man smirked, "Come with us if you please…Sir."

Frayne glanced at the lighted rooms behind him, then closed the door firmly and clamped the metal circles about his wrists.

"Lead the way, gentlemen."

Adam was roused from a fitful slumber by his jailer bursting into his cell, flanked by two heavyset guards.

"Up." The man commanded, fury etched into every crevice of his face.

Perplexed, Adam stumbled to his feet, squaring his shoulders and readying himself to face whatever was to come.

"Arms forward." The jailer demanded, reaching impatiently for Adam's wrists. The guards held him by each arm while his keeper fussed about freeing him from his bonds, each rigid movement a picture of affronted dignity.

"Out." The little man ordered, and Adam was dragged, silently but roughly, from the small room and out into the prison corridors.

"If I am to be hanged, I wish first to speak to a priest." He addressed the man on his right. "Where am I being taken?" He turned to the one on his left.

"Out." The man said before unceremoniously thrusting Adam out of the prison doors and closing them loudly behind him. Adam stared for a moment, bemused, at the building behind him and then turned and rushed away through the streets towards home.

The sun had barely crested the horizon, and Adam reached Dahlia's shop just as the city began to wake around him. He pounded relentlessly on the door until its owner opened it, her pale face peering out at him with an expression of mingled fear and hope.

"Adam!"

"Where is Frayne?" He brushed past her into the shop where Farrah was already waiting. "Where is Frayne?" He repeated, more forcefully this time.

Farrah stared at him in confusion. "He had a plan to rescue you. He went to gather some information, but he should have returned by now. We assumed he was delayed, but Devin went to find him…" she trailed off, a look of panic crossing her face.

"Adam?" Dahlia moved forward to embrace him, but he shook his head,

"Something is wrong. They just threw me out of the prison. I thought they would send someone to follow me to get to Frayne, but there was no one."

The initial fear on Dahlia's face had not faded, "Perhaps you just did not see them, Adam. We should leave here for safety's sake."

At that moment, the door flew open again, and Devin

burst in, his face red with anger, "Frayne's in prison again. People say 'e was taken from 'ere last night." He stopped in shock when he noticed Adam standing before him. "What're you doing 'ere?"

Adam's look of shock matched Devin's, then gradually darkened into anger as realisation forced its way to the forefront of his mind, "'...so Judas kissed his master, and cried 'all hail!' when he meant all harm.'"

There was a moment of confused silence.

"You cannot be suggesting that Frayne was betrayed?" Farrah stared at him in bewilderment.

"How else would they have found him?" Adam's voice was flat.

She shook her head, flinging away the tears that had begun to spill over. "There are many ways, Adam, it makes no sense, what would we gain from giving him up?"

"Why else would I have been freed, Farrah?" his stare was cold with a barely checked rage.

Farrah's breath caught in her throat as she turned to look at him, and the words that she had heard the day before seemed to echo once more in her ears, "I cannot stand back and let him die. If it is in my power to act Farrah, I will do it, no matter the cost, or I will die with him".

"Dahlia?" The word seemed to choke her as she looked towards her friend.

Dahlia's face was an image of triumphant misery, "I tried to tell you, Farrah," her voice was small but strong. "I tried to tell you that I could not face this."

"And I can?"

"Yes."

Farrah stared at her, silently aghast, but Dahlia shook her head, "They swore not to harm him. Extended incarceration will be his only punishment."

"And you believed them?" Devin was incredulous.

"No," Adam took a step away from her. "She did not believe them. She simply did not care."

"Please, Adam, I did this because I love you, because I know that I cannot live without you. I saved you in the only way that I could. Frayne would understand. He would have given himself up had he the opportunity to save you."

They stared at Dahlia then, none trusting themselves to answer her.

"Farrah, please, you cannot tell me that you would not have done the same, sacrificed one of us for Frayne." Misery now stood aside as desperation crept into Dahlia's voice.

"No, I would not have."

Farrah looked on the verge of collapsing, and Devin moved forward to take her arm gently.

"We were a family, Dahlia, the only family any of us had. Frayne loved you as though you were his sister. That is a bond that should never have been broken." She allowed Devin to lead her towards a chair. Bright tears stood out in the large man's eyes, but he held his words tightly within himself.

"Adam?" Dahlia was shaking now, pleading.

"Frayne would have found a solution. There was no need for your interference."

His callous tone ignited a flash of anger within her, "Frayne is not God Adam! He has his limits. He could not save you, but I could!"

"Yes, Frayne has his limits, but he had not reached them then. He has reached them now though, Dahlia."

Dahlia shrank back from his unforgiving stare. She glanced towards Farrah and Devin for any glimmer of comfort, but Farrah's eyes were hollow, empty, and Devin resolutely gazed at the floorboards by his feet, unwilling to show the cracks that were now spreading across his heart.

Their coldness staggered her, and she realised in one overwhelming moment that by her own hand, she had driven everyone she loved away from her. I believe that knowledge was too great for Dahlia to bear. Deep within herself, something shattered, and the mask of angelic goodness fell away. The darkness that had plagued her in the nights now awoke in the light of day. A dreadful bitterness surged within her, and with a wry smile, she turned to Adam.

"What Adam, no Shakespeare? No pretty words to allay the pain and lend drama to the scene? No cursing the stars, the fates, or the woman who loves you?"

"You have killed my brother."

Simple words spoken with unbearable pain. There are times when such words, adorned with nothing but agony, cut deeper than the most eloquent discourse ever can. That single phrase etched itself into Dahlia's heart and remained. Some wounds never heal.

They left then. They could have raged, cursed, and wept, but the three were numb, shattered. Devin raised his eyes only once to catch a final glimpse of the daughter who had broken his heart. They did not seek Dahlia out after that.

CHAPTER TWENTY-FIVE

They found themselves together at their old inn. It had been their first true home within the city, back when a life of larceny had seemed a grand adventure. The small building had always been a comfortable refuge amidst the chaos of their lives, a place of safety, of trusted friends, and good drink. Yet, somehow, the familiarity of that haven now served only to highlight the gaping holes that had opened in their lives. The chairs in the taproom where Frayne and Dahlia once would have sat now stood empty, never to be filled again.

Farrah and Adam sat in dismal silence, watching as Devin stood at the bar in a quiet conference with the innkeeper.

"Farrah, I am sorry."

She paused for a moment, surprised by Adam's words, but then shook her head slowly. "No, Adam, you have lost as much as I have, perhaps more."

"Perhaps I brought it upon myself. I am 'one who loved not wisely, but too well.'"

A dejected silence descended again.

"If he dies, Adam, how am I to live? As long as I remember him, I cannot go on without him."

Adam smiled, but the melancholy remained. "You will not forget him, Farrah, but you will continue on. You will grieve, but once the time for grieving has passed, you will take his name down from your lips and tuck it safely into your heart. There it will remain, a gentle pain to remind you of joys passed and a beautiful memory to carry you through to eternity. That piece of him will remain in you all your life, until your heart, and his name with it, turn to dust, and you find yourself standing beside him once again."

Farrah shook her head, "He cannot die, Adam, he cannot."

"I've got us rooms." Devin fell heavily into a chair beside Adam, "Innkeeper wouldn't let me pay. A right good man is Thomas."

He sighed, then forced a slight smile onto his face as he saw Bessie, the innkeeper's young daughter, approaching their table, an overflowing mug clasped tightly in her small hands. The girl's expression was sombre, her eyes devoid of the childish delight that normally suffused them. It made her seem older somehow, though when Farrah looked at Bessie, she saw only the delighted creature adorned with lace, silk, and smudges of sugar that had stood by her side on the happiest day of her life. A film of tears washed over Farrah's eyes at the memory, but she smiled and took the proffered drink from the girl.

"Thank you, Bessie."

The three stared at their untouched drinks for a time, and then Devin cleared his throat, "We should go to the prison. You can wear disguises, but it won't matter. Pay them enough, and the guards won't touch us."

Adam nodded slightly in response. It was a risk, but wasn't everything else in their lives?

They did not linger at the inn after that but made their way hurriedly to the prison. As a precaution, Adam and Farrah made meagre attempts to conceal their identities but, as Devin had said, the guards cared little who visited their prison, provided they received ample compensation. When they reached Frayne's cell, they were granted an audience through a small, barred window, flanked on each side by an armed man.

Farrah was the first at the window and eagerly pressed her face to the bars to catch a glimpse of her husband. As soon as he saw Farrah, Frayne struggled up from where he had been sitting on the floor. He looked no worse considering his situation and smiled at Farrah with the same easy charm he had always possessed. His hands were manacled and chained to the floor, as were his feet, so he was forced to stop a metre from the doorway. Farrah glanced around the cell, surprised by the utter lack of furniture. There was no chair or chamberpot—not even a cot disturbed the room's emptiness.

"Your room is rather sparse, is it not, especially considering that you are the jailer's favourite guest?"

Farrah was painfully aware of the bars separating her from her husband and the two guards who stood nearby listening to her every word.

Frayne shook his head, "Alas, I have ruined all their fine furniture in the past, so they did not see fit to entrust me with more."

They both smiled, but the painful truth cut deeply at them—Frayne would not be held at the prison long enough to warrant any furniture. He leaned slightly into his chains, wishing more than anything he could be closer to her, if only for a moment.

"Farrah, if I die, I shall carry your name with me to heaven and present it before God and say to him, 'Please, watch over her especially until such a time as we might be together again'."

"And if you die and go to hell as is infinitely more likely, what then?" Farrah asked, arching her eyebrows.

"Then I shall see you there."

Frayne grinned, but his smile quickly faltered. Humour can only keep fear and grief at bay for so long.

"Farrah, if I do not make it out of this…"

She shook her head firmly, cutting off his words. "You shall, Frayne, you shall make it through, and we will return home, have ten children, and be happy for the rest of our lives."

Her words were an empty hope, she knew it as she spoke them, but behind them was a fire and a strength—the same strength that had carried Farrah's mother through the death of her husband. For a brief moment Frayne knew that, even without him, Farrah would find joy.

He smiled, "I will love you forever, Farrah."

The tears that had been gathering in her eyes spilt over and she could smile no longer.

"I will love you forever, Frayne."

Adam approached the window next, grief overwhelming the anger that had burned within him all day. For a long time, the two men could only stare at one another, then Frayne broke the silence.

"Dahlia?"

Adam nodded.

"I am sorry, Adam."

What more could be said?

Adam shrugged, "'She's gone, I am abused, and my relief must be to loathe her.'" His shoulders sagged, "But how can I loathe one whom I have loved for so long?"

"'We are not the first who with best meaning have incurred the worst.'"

Adam smiled slightly, "Do you remember what Shakespeare wrote after that?"

Frayne shook his head, "It's a miracle I remembered that much, Mate."

"'Come, let's away to prison. We two alone will sing like birds in the cage. When you ask my blessing, I'll kneel down and ask of you forgiveness. So we'll live, and pray, and sing, and tell old tales, and laugh at gilded butterflies, and hear poor rogues talk of court news, and we'll talk with them too—who loses and who wins, who's in, who's out—and take upon us the mystery of things as if we were God's spies. And we'll wear out in a walled prison packs and sects of great ones that ebb and flow by the moon.' That's been our life together, hasn't it? Living, praying, singing, telling old tales, laughing at the rich, thinking on life's mysteries, slipping in and out of prisons, and lasting, always lasting."

Frayne nodded, "Good lives we've had, really."

"Few could boast of better."

They settled into silence again.

"Don't loathe her, Adam, in that do not listen to Shakespeare. Find forgiveness, find love, and find happiness again. Live, for my sake."

Adam nodded. There was so much more that he wished to say, but at that moment, his words would not come. They were no longer needed. He and Frayne had spent their lives together saying all that needed to be said, and now, facing the end, they found solace in the silence between them, knowing that they were brothers still, and the only thing that could separate them was death.

Last came Devin. He smiled to see Frayne, though his heart was cracked within him.

"Fine mess we're in."

Frayne nodded, weariness slipping over his face.

"Thank you, Frayne."

Frayne looked up in surprise, "For what?"

"For saving my life. Don't think I would've made it without you and all the rest. You gave me something to live for."

Frayne smiled, "You are a good man, Devin. Cymbeline was right to see something in you."

Tears pricked at the large man's eyes, "Don't be afraid of death. It's just another step we all take, sooner or later. And don't be afraid of leaving 'er either." He glanced back towards Farrah, "We'll take care of 'er. She won't be alone."

"Thank you, Devin."

The two men nodded to each other once more, and then Devin turned away from the small window to where Adam and Farrah were waiting. They walked together slowly through the prison, back to the outside world, each holding their grief tightly against themselves, praying that the others would not see them break and that in their strength, their friends would find comfort.

CHAPTER TWENTY-SIX

The day of Frayne's execution was a glorious one. Golden shafts of sunlight pierced through the cloudy shroud that blanketed the city, sweeping aside the grey fog to reveal a perfectly blue sky beneath. At the first hint of dawn, birds began calling out from unseen perches, and a gentle summer breeze carried with it the comforting smell of baking bread. There was a holiday feeling in the air, and Frayne was at the centre of it all. By now, his name was known throughout the city. Men, women, and children awoke with excitement, delighted at the prospect of seeing such a famous man. It hardly seemed to matter to them that he was to die. In a way, it seemed to excite them further. How would he die? Would there be gallant speeches, final acts of bravery or defiance, a grand gesture of apology? And what would such a man look like? The young women, in particular, took great care in dressing that morning. A fine gentleman was to die, and perhaps theirs would be the last pretty face he saw.

The city was awash with romantic notions and exhilaration. Small children tugged impatiently at their parents' hands as thousands of men, women, and children jostled for a place among the crowds that had gathered to witness the death of a hero. Alone, scattered amongst the happy throng, were four people with heavy hearts in their chests. The rest of the crowd ignored them. Their misery had no place on such a momentous day.

A spectacular procession made its way throughout the city. Frayne was taken from the prison in a cart, his hands bound behind him, his head held high. Accompanying him was a City Marshal, mounted upon a beautiful horse, and stationed both before and behind the cart was a score of liveried men, their uniforms bright in the morning sunshine. There was no talk of heroes, demons, or liberators now. Frayne stood before the city, his myth stripped away to reveal a man—proud and strong, handsome and good—and it was his name alone that the multitudes chanted. He played his part well, nodding graciously to those he passed, never allowing a hint of fear to show on his face.

The cart came to a stop outside of an inn. It was tradition that a condemned man be allowed one final drink, and on such a day, the crowds would have demanded nothing less. Frayne stepped down from the cart of his own accord and was accompanied into the inn by liveried men and the cheers of onlookers. The inside of the building was cool, and a welcome respite from the noise of the streets.

Dozens of curious nobles gathered around the bar. Each had paid a small fortune to stand close to this famed man while the rest of the crowd waited outside. It could not escape notice that many of the gathered gentries were ladies, their faces artfully painted, throats adorned with flashing jewels, but Frayne paid them no heed. He strode assuredly to the bar where a young girl with brown curls waited, a cup of pale wine clutched in her hands.

Frayne bent slightly to accept the drink, "Thank you," he whispered.

The girl nodded back at him, but her expression remained strained, and tears began to gather at the corners of her eyes.

Frayne smiled, "None of that now." He winked at her and bowed deeply, "I am in your debt, Lady."

The girl offered him a watery grin and dipped into a quick bob before running behind the bar to where her father waited.

It was past noon by the time the procession reached the gallows. Vendors hawked their wares over the noise of the crowds, and the air filled with the smell of food as small parcels were passed from hand to hand. Frayne descended from the cart for the last time and climbed the stairs of the scaffold unaccompanied. He stood tall and unwavering as the noose slipped about his neck, and a hush seemed to fall over the city as the crowd waited eagerly to hear his last words.

He smiled at those gathered before him, "I shall not waste your time, good people, in asking for your pardon, for I made my choice in life and shall not recant it in death. I ask only that God forgive me for any wrongs I have committed against him and beg that he may receive my spirit with grace. And you dear people, may you find something in your own lives to bring you as much joy as I have found in mine own."

With that, he turned to his executioner and nodded, then, facing back towards his audience, took a deep breath as the lever was pulled and the ground opened beneath his feet.

The crowd stood in horrified silence. Frayne hung before them, but though his chest still rose and fell, he did not thrash or struggle, as slowly, the rope drew his life from him. He looked out at them stoically, passively, patiently waiting to greet Death. This was what they had come to see. They would tell their children about this for years to come—they had met a thief, a hero with otherworldly powers, so comfortable with Death that he could meet him without a fight.

Gradually, Frayne's eyes swept over those that had gathered before him. They paused for a moment on a face framed in long, dark hair. Although the young woman had once been strikingly beautiful, her features were now marred irreparably by guilt. Something within her seemed broken beyond repair—her eyes were imploring, and her mouth opened as if to utter a belated plea for forgiveness. Frayne's gaze did not linger. His eyes held no resentment or sense of betrayal, but they offered no hint of absolution either. They were empty, the light within them slowly fading.

As if by a great effort, his gaze continued to search the crowd until it finally came to rest on a face as familiar to him as his own. It wore a sombre look and reminded him again of a watch that had once been so precious to him—pale-faced, framed with gold. Its hands had marked the end of one life and the beginning of the next. And this face, Farrah's face, had been with him at the beginning of one life and was now with him at the end. Something about that seemed significant to Frayne, but his thoughts were floating away from him. There was no pain, only distance—a great distance pulling him far from the crowd before him. Still, he was anchored by the two dusty green eyes locked tightly with his. They were immeasurably beautiful, achingly familiar, but fading slowly away. Only one regret touched him: he was leaving her too soon, far too soon, but then that, too, was gone.

Deep within the gathered crowd, Farrah gazed steadily into Frayne's wavering eyes. She knew that his sight was flickering between her world and eternity, but still, he held on, and she refused to look away—choosing to believe her gaze alone held him to life. Death's cold hand was already painting upon the canvas of her heart—a familiar masterpiece of loss, pain, and overwhelming sorrow—but she would not allow tears to come, not yet. Nothing would obscure her last view of the man whose name was etched upon her very soul. Slowly, reluctantly, Frayne's eyes closed, and his breathing gently stilled. In the silence that followed, two silver rivers carved a pathway down Farrah's cheeks.

As Frayne's eyes closed, a ripple seemed to run through the crowd. The uncanny silence was broken, first by whispers and then by shouts, then as one, the throng surged towards the gallows. Frantically, the men in livery rushed forward to hold back the pressing masses, but their pikes could only restrain the mob for so long.

"Sir!" a young man ran from behind the scaffolding to where the City Marshall sat in bewilderment upon his horse, "Sir, they fear dissection. They want the body."

The Marshall shook his head, shock plain upon his face, "He must hang for fifteen minutes. It is far too soon to cut him down."

The young man blanched, "Sir, they will tear us to pieces if he hangs any longer. We must remove the body."

The Marshall looked in fear at the mob, "It is too soon…"

"I can fetch the doctor immediately. He can confirm the death, but Sir, we must leave now."

The Marshall nodded, emerging from his shock, "Fetch

the doctor and cut the body down. We cannot leave it for the mob to rally around, or next thing you know, we will have a riot on our hands."

The young man barely heard the end of his words before sprinting back to the top of the scaffolding and cutting Frayne's body down. A doctor was summoned, a dark, serious-looking man who felt Frayne's pulse and pronounced him dead. The body was hurriedly thrown onto the cart on which Frayne had arrived less than half an hour earlier.

"You," the Marshall grabbed the young man's shoulder as he hurried past him, "drive the cart to the churchyard and see that he is buried quickly. I will deal with this."

"Yes, Sir." the young man gasped, vaulting onto the cart and urging the horses into a trot. He turned back to see one of the liverymen go down and the crowd surge forward, but they were too late. Frayne was gone.

A few days later, a simple tombstone appeared in a quiet churchyard. It was, as Adam had once predicted, little more than a scrap of stone adorned with a few words. It read:

> "From this day to the ending of the world,
> But we in it shall be remembered—
> We few, we happy few, we band of brothers…"

CHAPTER TWENTY-SEVEN

Life moved on, as it always must. Grief is a shifting thing, and although time does not heal all wounds, it graces us with the numbness that we need to continue. After Frayne's execution, Farrah, Adam, and Devin left the city, each seeking a new beginning.

Farrah travelled south to a new country, far from the fear and the pain of her past. There, she found safety and a new home for herself and, six months later, for the daughter she had carried within her. Farrah named her Godiva, and together, they created a beautiful life.

With her money from her years of theft, Farrah bought an old country manor, one reminiscent of the home Frayne had gifted her after their wedding. It became a place of laughter and contentment for Farrah and her small family, and through the years was filled with friends and beautiful memories.

Through wealth and connections, Farrah became a Lady in her own right, as her mother had once dreamed she would be. As befitting her new station, she took great delight in hosting all manner of dances and dinners. The guests she welcomed into her halls were a far cry from the fashionable elite that found amusement in other fine homes. Farmers, smiths, bakers, servants, and their families paraded arm in arm across her dance floor, the laughter that tumbled from their lips adding light to her home. More than one motherless urchin found refuge in her house, a friend in her daughter, and a long-sought-after love in her embrace. In these children, she found the family Frayne had dreamed of them having and a lasting joy that had escaped her for so long.

Farrah's life continued with the same contentments and struggles as all others. She returned to the country of her birth many times to visit Adam and Devin, and as the years began to dull the sting of Dahlia's betrayal, Farrah found herself searching for news of her more and more. The bliss of the present reminded her of the goodness of the past, and though Dahlia had hurt her, Farrah still dreamed of seeing her sister again. Perhaps that is the nature of age. The wounds of our youth fade to pale lines, and we find ourselves desiring reconciliation before we walk into eternity. Although she searched for many years, Farrah never found her. It is my greatest hope that, somehow, despite the pain in her heart, Dahlia found peace.

As for Adam, his life, though not a long one, was lived wonderfully well. Following Frayne's execution, he travelled north to a new city where he opened his own theatre. It became a refuge for the orphaned and destitute—a place where they could learn a new trade and where, during their time on the stage, they could forget the darkness that coloured their pasts and enter a new world.

Adam created a place of magic where pain and ruthlessness were forgotten. To all those who came to his theatre, rich or poor, he offered respite and a new balm to soothe the wounds that the world inflicts upon us all.

Adam offered them words—his own beautiful words—spoken through the mouths of players who had risen from nothing to become princes, gods, and heroes on his stage.

Adam never married, though he had no shortage of proposals. He remained a lively, joyful man his whole life, but romance had lost its lustre for him. He visited Farrah many times over the years, but never once sought out Dahlia. I do not believe that he held any bitterness in his heart towards her. He had forged a new life for himself instead, one in which the griefs and regrets of the past were no longer needed.

Most telling, perhaps, were the words of his plays. One speech now stands out in my memory—a young man counselling his friend on the loss of his love: "Yes, for a time you shall suffer, but then you will begin a new life apart from her. You will remember how to live, to laugh, and most importantly, to love. The girl who once claimed your heart will become one more ghost wandering through the deep recesses of your memory, searching for a way out. Then, one day, that ghost will disappear and take the brokenness of your heart with her, and you shall move on."

Adam wrote about his friends. How I wish I could remember all his words now. They each appeared in his stories and plays in one guise or another. Frayne was a knight, a demon, a prince, and—on one memorable occasion—a lion. Farrah was a fairy or enchantress, never a mortal woman. Devin was always a giant, and Dahlia, though she never appeared as a character, was there too. In the early days, she was the grief, anger, sadness, and regret behind Adam's words. As time passed, she changed to a gentle longing, weaving through his character's speeches. As the years went on, however, she faded from the stage, as her hold on Adam's heart lessened and passed away.

When Death came for Adam, it did not find him alone as he had once feared. Adam died surrounded by friends who loved him. He had brought hope and joy into each of their lives, and when he had breathed his last, they gathered up his legacy and carried it out into the world with them. His name lives on in the theatres that he loved and on the tongues of great orators, but for me, Mr Simmons, Adam lives on in the rooftops and the narrow streets of his city. Although I have never believed in ghosts, it brings me much joy to look to my rooftop each day and imagine that a small figure stands there wreathed in the early morning mist, wild straw hair whipping about his face, feet bare despite the cold, and a laugh full of exhilaration dancing from his lips.

Now to Devin. Out of them all, it is for him that my heart breaks the most. He was a man of such goodness and compassion, yet so marred by the scars of life that the only lasting peace he found was in the embrace of Death. His end came at the hands of soldiers, though not in some great battle for life, limb, and glory, but in a fight for a single broken soul.

Devin had returned north after staying a while with Farrah and found himself wandering the streets of a new city, enjoying the quiet that comes before dawn. A garrison was stationed there, and Devin nodded courteously as he passed soldier after soldier, some returning to their beds and others just rising, the marks of sleep still heavy upon their faces. The men were resplendent in their uniforms, but something was unnerving about their presence there, and Devin found a growing tension entering his limbs. There had been a time when he had served and found glory in fighting for the crown, but that time had long passed, and the faces he saw about him now seemed younger and more uncertain than those he remembered.

Two soldiers stumbled from a bar, still drunk, though the time for drinking was long past. With an unsteady gait, they made their way hurriedly down the street but halted when they noticed a small beggar girl asleep in a doorway. I do not know what it was about the wretched figure that roused the men to ire, but she awoke to a flurry of abuse more painful than she had ever known before. Devin saw the flashing boots and the tiny figure curled up in fear and agony before them. He had spoken once of seeing his wife's face whenever the anger came for him, but this time, as the crimson darkness filled his eyes, there was no vision of serenity to hold him back. The soldiers fell before Devin like broken dolls.

Gently, he raised the girl to her feet and brushed away her tears with his calloused fingertips, "There, you're safe now." He smiled at her, and I can imagine that at that moment, his face—strong and ferocious, sculpted to wear pain—changed, as it always had whenever he had looked upon Farrah, Dahlia, or Bessie, and in them, seen his daughter.

No man takes favourably to seeing his companions struck down in the street, and Devin was soon surrounded by a group of soldiers who had seen him standing by the unconscious bodies of their friends. The girl ran from them but paused at the mouth of an alleyway to see what would become of her rescuer. Rage filled Devin once more, and he struck hard at the men who would take his life for the sake of their comrades' dignity.

He saw the girl hesitate and turn back to him, saw the pain and the shock in her eyes that welled up into angry tears. I know that when he finally fell, it was not the poor wretch's face before him that he saw, but one wreathed in celestial light that turned from fear to amazement and finally to joy when she saw her beloved Papa was coming home at last.

I do believe that since his wife's death, Devin had existed with one foot in this world and the other in the next, pulled between life and love. So, when at last his end came, I am sure that it was with a grateful sigh of relief that he took the single step into eternity. I may not be sure of the rest, but I do not doubt that Devin was accompanied by angels when he departed this world. Despite his unholy anger, there was righteous goodness within him that destined him for paradise.

Finally, Mr Simmons regarding Frayne, I can offer you this hope. Frayne lived his life fearlessly, as though he and Death had reached some agreement long ago that left him free to tempt fate. He had faced his end many times, but in each instance, it seemed that Death had chosen to look the other way. Frayne's plans, though always far-fetched, rarely failed, and I can assure you, he would not have gone submissively to the gallows unless he had some hope of rescue.

There are cases, rare but not unheard of, of men who hung for the allotted fifteen minutes, were cut down, and then sprang back up again to face their executioner. Furthermore, there are poisons that can slow a man's heart almost to a stopping point and doctors who can restore a dead heart to beating. Frayne hung for no more than ten minutes, so he had a greater chance than many. Still, I speak only of vague possibilities, Mr Simmons—whether Frayne truly lived or died is not in my power to tell. All I may say with certainty is that a stone stands for him in a quiet churchyard, and somewhere in the world, a heart still carries his name. To be honest, the idea that Frayne survived his hanging is a far-fetched hope, but still, it is one that I choose to hold on to, for it is hope that carries us onwards.

I remain,
Sincerely and Gratefully Yours

EPILOGUE

Somewhere, a clock was chiming. It was a piece of familiar music, deep and stately, that conjured up images of proud grandfather clocks, worn leather sofas, and the rich scent of cigar smoke. The melody seemed out of place in this room with its bright fluorescent lights and hardwood floors. The chairs, metal frames with padded seats, had provided the illusion of comfort when I first walked in, but now sitting, I decided that a leather sofa, no matter how worn, would be much preferred. I have always hated those padded metal chairs.

"Are you ok?"

My mother's low voice pulled my focus back and I looked at the small woman behind the desk. She had blonde hair and large glasses and was methodically typing information into my grandfather's death certificate. I glanced over at my mother sitting next to me, nodded, and then let my focus wander again. Birth, marriage, and death—three pieces of paper to mark that wonderful man's existence. Three pieces of paper and a little plaque laid in a pretty garden for passersby to read. Not that they would read it.

He was a stranger to them, and passersby are too preoccupied with their own busy lives to stop and read a stranger's name. My grandfather would have read it, though, had it belonged to another man.

Grandfather was the sort of person who moved slowly through the world, spending much of his time within his own mind and living for the little mysteries that life throws our way. His one true passion was manuscripts, old manuscripts that spoke of other people's lives.

Grandfather's passion for documents went through many different phases throughout his life. When he was younger, he collected records of court cases settled long ago. Then he moved on to family trees, historical recordings, poems when he met my grandmother, and then letters. When I was born, he began collecting stories—just short ones, written on faded pages by men now turned to dust. As I grew older, he read them to me, and we speculated about the figures who wrote them.

My favourite was always the letter to Mr Simmons. As a child, I loved the adventure in it. My grandfather and I would build prisons with tables, chairs, and blankets and then, together, we would plot our escapes. It's not hard to remember him like that, his knees pulled up to his ears and a grin creeping across his face, as together we crouched beneath the dining room table while my grandma, the jailer, got closer and closer.

As I grew older, I became fascinated by the characters. I desperately wanted the story to be true, and not just another sentimental fairytale. But though Grandfather and I searched, we found no other record of Frayne, Farrah, Adam, Devin, or Dahlia. Unwilling to admit that the letter was nothing more than a lovely story, we decided that the author had used assumed names for them all for their protection. Still, with little else to go on, we both knew we had no hope of finding the truth.

Over time, I admit that I lost interest in it all. I grew up and moved away, I entered the workforce, and sought to quash my sentimental nature that my grandfather called "endearing", and I, "romantic, childish, foolishness". I started my own life and found my own passions, different from those of my grandfather. I am ashamed to say that I neglected him somewhat. I called him from time to time and sent him a card on his birthday, but I rarely visited or read the old books he told me about over the phone. I was one of the passersby, so caught up in my own life that I didn't make time to stop, didn't have time for the sorts of people who found fun hiding beneath dining room tables. A part of me just stopped caring until now.

My grandfather died two days before I found myself in that cold room with the horrible chairs. He was gone, but he left me with his collection of documents, lovingly gathered over almost a century of life. It was lovely but overwhelming, and a piece of me chafed against the idea of caring for such a vast treasure. I had little interest in the papers now, though I had once loved them, but to sell them would be to discard the one piece of my grandfather now left to me.

I left the records office feeling like a great weight had dropped on my shoulders.

"Don't worry, Love." My mum whispered to me. "You can keep the papers at our house. We have space in the loft. Box them up and bring them over when you have the chance."

So that is what I did. It took forty-six boxes and three weeks, but Grandfather always kept his documents well organised, so it was no great chore. Out of all the hundreds of records, stories, poems, and letters, I kept just one—the letter to Mr Simmons.

I read it many times over the ensuing years. It was like having a piece of my grandfather with me still. So many of my childhood memories were tied up in those faded pages, but I found something else in it too, though I can't say exactly what it was, perhaps a sense of encouragement. The more I read it, the more I found myself pulled into the mystery of the letter again. Had the writer just been an imaginative old lady, or was there some truth to her story?

Since I had previously had no success tracking down the characters, I decided to search for places instead. I began by looking for a gravestone etched with Shakespeare's immortal words, "From this day to the ending of the world, but we in it shall be remembered—we few, we happy few, we band of brothers…". Finding no such stone, I started searching for a record of the inn, then Dahlia's shop, then Mrs Alves' house. I was amazed by how many similar places exist in this country.

Finally, I turned my efforts towards finding the manor house Frayne bought Farrah after their wedding. The letter had this to say on the subject, "Frayne and Farrah travelled north for several days until they reached a large house tucked quietly away in a valley beside a lake. It was a lovely thing and Frayne's wedding gift to Farrah. The day they arrived, the wind was still, and the lake transformed into glass. From a distance, the house, so close to the banks, appeared to be resting on the edge of a fallen silk of sky. As they grew closer, the reflection of the house materialised in the lake, and it looked as though two similar worlds had drawn together and, for a fleeting moment, were separated only by a thin blade of green.

It was an enchanted place, edged with orchards and guarded by forests—cut off from the world and adorned with the most beautiful memories. It was a home of laughter and happy secrets. At its centre, it held a promise—that one day, when the excitement of their lives in the city had faded, Frayne and Farrah would return here together, to walk hand in hand through the orchards once more, and sit, arms entwined, upon the wall of their secret garden, smiling as the last rays of the setting sun faded from their sight."

It was not much to go on, but after years of careful research, I found it. I cannot describe quite how it felt to look upon that house. It was like finding a pot of gold at the end of a rainbow and shaking hands with the red-haired man who guarded it. It was just as the letter had described—a few days' ride from our biggest city, sheltered in a valley and obscured from the world by thick forests.

On the day I first beheld it, the wind blew mercilessly, and as it filtered through those ancient trees, it seemed to lend them a voice. All around me, they sighed as though bemoaning a past forgotten to all but them. The manor still stood on the banks of the lake, but the wind that cried through the trees also flung the lake into a fury—the churning waters revealing a shattered reflection of a faded house.

As I walked its halls, the rotting wood and coatings of dust seemed to fade into the background. There was a feeling of joy contained within its walls and lingering laughter. The letter had spoken of Frayne and Farrah adorning the house with beautiful memories, and I could almost believe that they lingered there still, just awaiting the right pair of eyes to notice them again.

I wandered, alone, through the overgrown orchards and eventually came to a walled garden. I circled the stone walls until I found a small rotting doorway overgrown with vines. With much effort, I forced my way inside to behold a tangled mass of uprooted paving stones and overgrown weeds smothering all remaining vestiges of the garden's beauty. I carefully picked my way through to the far wall, where I paused to survey the dying garden. Beside me, two slender trees grew upward, reaching beyond the crumbling stone walls to the blue sky above. They grew so close together that their longest branches almost brushed against each other. I watched as the setting sun slowly painted the sky in soft pink and gold. The shadows began to lengthen, and the two trees seemed to stretch out their branches further as the last rays of the fading sun gently caressed their leaves.

AUTHOR'S NOTE

Although the characters in this book are entirely fictional, Frayne's many escapes were inspired by those of Jack Sheppard, a notorious thief who operated in London in the early 1700s. Sheppard was imprisoned five times in 1724 and escaped four times using the methods described in this book.

Sheppard was arrested for the first time in April of 1724. He was informed on by his brother, then betrayed by James Sykes, a thief in the employ of the notorious "Thief-Taker General", Jonathan Wild. Sheppard was imprisoned in a cell on the top floor of St. Giles' Roundhouse. He had an old razor in his pocket and used it to cut out the stretcher of a chair. He used the piece of wood to batter through the roof and used the bed in the cell to catch the falling rubble so that it would not make a noise as it dropped to the floor.

Unfortunately, a falling tile struck a man in the street below, who alerted the guard and a crowd of passers-by. Before the jailers could reach his cell, Sheppard fashioned a rope from his bedsheets and used it to lower himself to the churchyard below. When he reached the street, he joined the crowd and shouted that he could see the prisoner in the shadows on the roof.

Sheppard's second arrest took place a month later when he was caught trying to pick a pocket. He was visited in prison by his mistress, Elizabeth Lyon, who was a prostitute and a known criminal. Lyon was recognised and imprisoned in the same cell as Sheppard. They were then moved to the New Prison in Clerkenwell. A few days later, they escaped by filing through their manacles, removing a bar from their window, using their bedsheets as a rope to descend to the ground, and then escaping through the prison gate.

By this point, Sheppard's criminal abilities had earned the admiration of Wild. Wild wanted to partner with Sheppard to keep him under control, but he refused. Wild determined that Sheppard would be better off in prison, so he met with Elizabeth Lyon and plied her with drinks until she gave up his whereabouts. He was arrested again in July by one of Wild's subordinates.

Sheppard was held at Newgate Prison, tried, and sentenced to death. On the last day of August, he escaped again. He managed to loosen an iron bar in the window used by guards and visitors to look into the cell. Lyon and another woman visited him and distracted the guards while he removed the bar, climbed through the opening, and left the prison disguised in women's clothing.

Just over a week later, Sheppard was discovered by a posse, arrested, and returned to the condemned cell at Newgate Prison. The guards stopped two escape attempts and transferred Sheppard to the prison's strongroom. He was put in leg irons that were chained to two metal staples on the floor and secured with a horse padlock. Sheppard opened the padlock with a small nail and freed himself from his restraints, but it wasn't long before his jailers caught him wandering about his cell. Sheppard was secured to the floor once more and placed in handcuffs to prevent any further escape attempts.

On 15th October, Wild was attacked in court by a past associate of Sheppard's. The assault caused an uproar that spread to Newgate Prison and continued through the night. Sheppard took advantage of the disturbance, which distracted his keepers. He used his teeth to remove his handcuffs, then managed to twist a small iron link off the chain that held his legs to the floor. He made a hole in the cell's chimney and used the chain link to wrench out the iron bar that blocked his passage. Then, as described in this book, he broke through six locked doors and made his way to the roof. He returned to his cell once to retrieve a blanket, which he used to drop onto an adjoining house. Sheppard entered the building via the garret door, but finding the house's occupants still awake, he remained in the garret for three hours, then hurried down the stairs and out the front door, leaving it open behind him.

Sheppard was arrested again two weeks later. He had spent the day parading about the neighbourhood with a new mistress, poorly disguised as a gentleman, and drinking to excess. He was placed in the Middle Stone room of Newgate, closely observed, and held down by three hundred pounds of iron restraints. Sheppard refused to take a deal which would have granted him a reduced sentence in exchange for naming his associates. He was then sentenced to death.

On Monday, 16th November 1724, Jack Sheppard was taken to Tyburn to be hanged. He had hidden a penknife on his person and intended to cut his ropes on the way to the gallows and escape, but the implement was found just before he left the prison. Sheppard was paraded through the streets and taken to a tavern for a final drink before being led to the gallows. He had one last plan of escape. Sheppard's friends were waiting nearby to steal his body away as soon as it was cut down and take it to a doctor in the hopes that he could be revived. After hanging for fifteen minutes, Sheppard's body was cut down, but the watching crowd, fearing dissection, surged forward to stop him from being removed. His friends were unable to reach him, and his body was recovered much later and buried.

Throughout his life, Sheppard undertook almost every method of thievery. He began by stealing two silver spoons from a tavern, then moved on to house burglary, pickpocketing, and highway robbery. His life was one of vice and hedonism, but his youth, good looks, loyalty to his associates, disinclination to violence, and dramatic escapes made him a hero. His life and escapades have been celebrated in plays, books, engravings, songs, and films for the past three hundred years.

An account of Sheppard's actions can be read in *A Narrative of all the Robberies, Escapes, &c. of John Sheppard: Giving an Exact Description of the Manner of his Wonderful Escape From the Castle in Newgate and of the Methods he took afterward for his Security*. This biography is thought to have been ghostwritten by Daniel Defoe and endorsed by Sheppard. It was first printed and sold by John Applebee in 1724.

Made in the USA
Columbia, SC
21 February 2024